To D.J. from —
the best wishes
Ja[...]

to my favorite DJ,
Love always Sasha

Revenge of Underwater Man

The Richard Sullivan Prize in Short Fiction

Editors
William O'Rourke and Valerie Sayers

1996, *Acid*, Edward Falco
1998, *In the House of Blue Lights*, Susan Neville
2000, *Revenge of Underwater Man*, Jarda Cervenka

Revenge of Underwater Man

and Other Stories

Jarda Cervenka

University of Notre Dame Press
Notre Dame, Indiana

Copyright 2000 by
University of Notre Dame Press
Notre Dame, IN 46556
All Rights Reserved
Manufactured in the United States of America

Library of Congress Cataloging-in-Publication Data
Cervenka, Jarda.
    Revenge of Underwater Man and other stories / Jarda Cervenka.
        p. cm. — (Richard Sullivan prize in short fiction)
    ISBN 0-268-04000-1 (cloth : alk. paper) — ISBN 0-268-04001-X (pbk. : alk. paper)
    I. Series
PS3553.E84 R4 2000
813'.54—dc21   99-089196

∞ *The paper used in this publication meets the minimum requirements of the American National Standard for Information Sciences—Permanence of Paper for Printed Library Materials, ANSI Z39.48-1984.*

Contents

The Demise of Decathlon Man   1

The Killing of He-Who-Is-Without-Shadow   13

What I Will Do!   21

And Then There Were None   31

Hearts   41

Revenge of Underwater Man   43

Billy's Last Smoke   57

Yoroshiku   63

Ladies of the Brussels Night   73

On Brainwaves of Memory   85

Romancing "Platino"   93

African Apology   99

Report on the State of Angels   109

How I Came to the Feast   115

Acknowledgements

Not being possessed by the relentless drive of high achievers, I have continued writing for two reasons: I liked my first book and wanted to write a better one, and most importantly, I have been constantly encouraged. My encouragers I thank from the depth of my heart.

I am grateful to my son Vojta for carrying my book with him to faraway windsurfing races, and to my daughter Tereza for careful editing of each story. And special thanks and love to Sasha, my girl, who was without the slightest doubt that I would be published again, and designed the beautiful cover for this book. She actually helped me to travel, alone and often, to distant and suspicious destinations.

I'd like to express my gratitude to those friends who gave me hope by expressing their liking of my fables and plots: Jakub Tolar, Jan and Karla Triska, Marilyn Gorlin, Jiri Ruzicka, Patricia Hampl, Wally Burgdorf, Bob Buhrer, Esther Wattenberg, Jana Knitlova, Anezi Okoro, Yuichi Seki, Bob Shestak, many others, and the gentle friends of my kids.

Also it should be noted that the following stories contained in this volume have been published elsewhere:

"Hearts" in *Blue Jacket*, Niigata, Japan, 1996.

"On Brainwaves of Memory" in *Full Circle Nineteen*, anthology by Guild Press, Minneapolis, Minnesota, 1998.

"The Killing of He-Who-Is-Without-Shadow" in *Exploration 98*, University of Alaska Press, Juneau, Alaska, 1998.

"African Apology" in *Rag Mag*, Black Hat Press, Goodhue, Minnesota, Vol. 6, No. 2, 1999.

"Billy's Last Smoke" in *Notre Dame Review*, No. 9, 2000.

Revenge of Underwater Man

The Demise of Decathlon Man

*Port Moresby,
Papua-New Guinea,
"Sepik Pepik's Bar"*

"But I need all the dough, now," he told me, snapping his fingers and softening the demand with a smile that parted his three-colored beard. "All of it. Sorry."

"The full payment? Wouldn't it be right if you get half now and half when you bring me back?"

"Yeah, you would think so. But, you see, when I fly to the backcountry the rules change. That's how it is."

I knew I had zero chance to bargain, and he knew it, too. He took a sip and wiped the foam off his mustache. He explained: "Two reasons for it. First, it is tough to land up in the Highlands; you need too much luck, and to be absolutely frank with you, I don't trust those people up there. Some bad habits there, still." He stared at the masks and the imitation smoked head above the bar. "You might not even make it back out of the jungle, my friend. I am just trying to be frank, that's all."

He looked back at me with sympathy, perhaps. "And the second reason is that there is only one, single chopper here in Moresby—and you know who flies it. Me, number one. So what I say goes. You take it, or leave it."

"Can't argue about that," I said.

"No, you can't argue about that." He was a tough sonofabitch, but, in a way, he was right. I would have preferred a little pleasanter fellow though. On the other hand, everybody knew that you could not get a better helicopter pilot north of Torres Straight.

It was his Vietnam experience, and he was quite nostalgic about it. He flew three whole tours in the Land of the Big PX. First, he piloted the workhorse UH-1C, the Huey. ("Slickdrivers they called us. Slick? It was either slick—or bodybag, m'boy.") Then he'd realized his dream to become the "skypilot" of the assault helicopter, the Cobra. ("When we let scream-off those rocket launchers and all the guns and blasted rock-and-roll over the rumble—what a rush! Unbelievable.") When all was over, he returned to the States.

"Took a peek and didn't like what I saw. No friendships, you know, no real action, you know what I mean. And so I went back to Asia. Raided Borneo, Irian, Melanesia—you name it. Here, in Papua, I like it all right. Still pretty wild and free, and guys like you help me to save some dough, and maybe I'll try the States some day again. Fly a chopper for some hospital or for one of them weather stations. I don't know."

He lighted a cigarette, crumpled the empty box, and threw it at the barman, who caught it in the air. "Got me a girlfriend now. Half-breed. Good woman."

The next morning we roared up into the dirty sky and followed the river upstream. Sometimes the hills moved so near to us you could see the birds in panic diving between the treetops. I did not blame them; I panicked a few times too, when we got so close that I could identify the genus and even the species of orchids in bloom. Finally, after the stream changed from brown chocolate to tea, he found a landing place on a sandy bar piercing a bend of the river, next to a denuded slope covered with ferns. We touched down gently, like thousands of pounds of damselfly. He did not cut the motor; the rotor made the sand fly.

"Two weeks, same place, same time!" he screamed. "Be sure to count the days right! Good luck. You'll need it!" He threw a six-pack of Fosters on the sand and went straight up, taking with him civilization as we know it. He left behind the silence that sounds like loneliness, and little me, sitting on my backpack.

That same day the diminutive naked people emerged from the bush, wary at first, like me. I was discovered by the tribe of local (ex-?) headhunters and settled on the hard split-bamboo floor with the Chief's family, amidst many wide smiles. The adventures had begun, causing every day to account for about two weeks of life in Connecticut. I liked that.

By the end of the week, news had arrived that a white man was coming up the river. White man. It was a big and rare event causing people to move faster with agitation, without direction. Soon, I shook hands with surprised Jindra.

In his fifties, he was in admirable condition except for his peeling raw forehead and a few tropical ulcers on his shins. He was one of the truest travelers, a man who has lived everywhere with a home nowhere. In those few days he stayed in the village, he told me many love stories and narrated events both believable and unbelievable. What sounded like high adventure to me seemed commonplace to him, and common experiences he considered adventures. He was a laid-back, pleasant fellow who cooked for himself on a miniature gas stove, the kind that mountain climbers use. He was omnivorous in his interests. Natives and all the oddities they performed, soil composition, birds (a disaster with me); he knew beetles by their Latin names and plants by the language of Papuans. He did not waste words or sentences; he did everything with deliberation and precision in his movements.

Before he would lean on a tree trunk, he never failed to check for ants. Before he would put on his canvas boots, he checked for scorpions. Entering a thicket, he would pause first, inspecting for a tree snake. He never slapped an insect landing on the back of his neck—he shooed it away. He peeled all fruit carefully (and still had to admit to chronic diarrhea), but he drank from jungle creeks, always followed with a smacking sound of gustatory delight. I watched him and learned. Even that smack.

Besides the stove, he carried a gold-panning dish. I knew there was gold in them thar hills, upstream, and asked about it. But Jindra avoided the aswer and said that he was looking for the world's largest butterfly, a ten-inch wingspan. He hoped Papuans could shoot it down with a bow and arrow for him. *Ornithoptera alexandrae.*

"Yap, alexandrae." He paused, his face smiling now. "Alexandra. I used to know one; she was beautiful. Blond, braided ponytail, thick like this forearm. Her mammae were the consistency of cartilage and in dimensions that dreams are made of. And her soul, my friend: gentle, generous." He hung his head in his special way, a little sideways. "I almost fell in love, then, I did."

So no gold? Ha! We left it at that.

His face carried the signatures of long stays in the tropics: bundles of wrinkles fanning from the outer corners of his eyes like clumps of miniature reeds, a map of sun blotches on his cheeks, and a nose-ridge marmorated in a nondescript pattern of browns and maroons.

Each of his eyes was of a different color, but this couldn't be attributed to the influence of an exotic sun; it was a developmental trait encoded in his chromosomes. It took me days before I noticed.

When he laughed, all his facial structures conspired together to a spastic sort of grin with clenched teeth, which was smile-inducing to observe. Contagious. When he did not laugh or talk, when he was unobserved, he kept the corners of his mouth downward, carp-like, and his eyebrows up high, which gave him a strange expression of surprised sadness. He could snap out of it in a second.

"You look sort of down, Jindra," I asked once. He had been staring at the river for a long while, motionless. "Anything wrong?"

"The river," he mumbled. He gave me a glance, shook his head and moved away, sideways—like a crab. I hadn't an idea about who he was, about his private soul. Not a clue. Till his last night.

The evening before his departure we made a little campfire by the river's bend, drank the Chief's banana "beer" and smoked, and listened to the roaring lullaby composed for the jungle. We pissed into the river in duo, threw sticks at the flashlight eyes of a crocodile across the stream. "Sometimes I get tired of roaming about," Jindra told me, crunching his dying pipe between his teeth so hard it vibrated a little. "I want to settle down somewhere. You know—like to stay put. Get me a nice lady, just fucking live a little." I asked him about the place he would choose to settle down. He has seen lot of places.

"The country doesn't matter that much. I hate countries and nations and that kind of bullshit," he said, taking his pipe out of his mouth and looking somewhere at the treetops still faintly outlined by the remnants of the day. "I'd like a place, you know, where I can dive into a pub in the evening. I would enter, and people sitting there would turn around. Some would raise their hand, would smile. They would holler, 'Jindra is here! Hey, Jindra came!' They would pull up chairs for me. I wouldn't know which one to take. I wouldn't know which one."

He paused, looked embarrassed a little. His eyes seemed full of wetness, but there was no smoke from the fire to cause it. He looked for the matches which lay on the sand right in front of him. "Shit, that is the place I would like to settle down." He shook his head as if not believing his divulgence, and added in a mocking voice with an exaggerated foreign accent, "Hey, Jindra is here!" Then he tilted his head to the side and bent it down. I changed the topic rapidly to avoid emotion. He did not fool me with his mockery.

I have since remembered every one of his words. Every one. He left me a homemade pipe of mangrove burl and a bag of seeds from a hallucinogenic vine. He disappeared up the river the next day. Alone.

There are bad rapids up there, and hostile folks who stick to some of the old, unpleasant dietary traditions. I don't know.

I am a multimillionaire. But no worry, I am not one of those hardworking financiers, determined go-getters. Every dollar, millions of them, came to me by way of inheritance, all the greenbacks with a picture of a smiling god on them. I have never worked a day for wages in my life. Even the toil of management of my funds and assets, as well as the anonymous charities, is done by my trustworthy managers. The riches have brought me freedom, above all. When I contemplate my destiny, the freedom part comes always to my mind. It makes me cheerful, even if it doesn't lead anywhere—it is what feels good. The elimination of the possibility of failure.

I used to ask myself, *"What am I good for, like for mankind, where lies my expertise,"* but by now it has become clear to me. I am a specialist in two subspecialities: the sporting life and living in many houses. While my admiration for top amateur athletes dates back to my wonderful childhood, only later did I develop this feeling of kinship with them. Like me, they behave as if they have inherited financial security, devoting all their energy and superhuman efforts to improve their speed or strength, with a disregard for the common sense of their fellow citizens.

While things have been changing lately, marathon runners, sprinters, and decathlonists still strive towards only one goal in their single-mindedness: to shorten their time for a distance, to increase their strength for an Olympic medal. I, myself, am a short fellow, balding already. But my muscles are delineated with the same sharpness and tension one admires on Florentine David, and more, I dare to say. This physique did not come with my inheritance; I had to build it with considerable effort. But that is another story.

As I have mentioned, I delight in living in many houses. My top three favorites, each one in a different world, are my houses on Gore Island, in Prague, and in Key West, Florida. I remembered the words of Jindra from Papua when I bought the first house abroad—on Gore. Gore is a speck of an island off the coast of West Africa, a short boatride from Dakar, Senegal. The island has gained infamy and notoriety for its fort-like structure on the eastern shore, near the landing. There, slaves used to be herded and stored by their black slavers (forgotten now, somehow), to be sold later to "white ships" that carried them to the Americas and the Caribbean. It is an interesting place, visited by tourists and "roots-seekers," whom I avoid, save for an occasional fair

The Demise of Decathlon Man   5

maiden who might seek Coca-Cola in the nearby shack with refreshments and fake, black shoe-polished, "ebony" carvings (the only eatery on the island).

My house on Gore reminds me of a gigantic cubic boulder. It is over two hundred years old and built of rock, with spacious rooms and ceilings as high as the sky. The walls are massive, two feet thick, and the windows are tall but narrow, to keep the noise outside and the coolness inside. The antique furniture is arrayed sparsely in the vast spaces to enhance my feeling of freedom. The paintings and sculptures are a mix of abstract and romantic, pleasing to my eye.

It stands near the village square, which is roofed over by an immense baobab tree under which old men, ethnic Woloff, gather. I have never seen them coming or leaving; they seem to be rooted into that red, hardened clay, like the baobab. They have their tiny portable stools to sit on, and homemade pipes and, sometimes, a bottle of palm brew to go around. And, always, many a story, narrated before. The stories are aged like red Bordeaux, and like the wine from Haut-Medoc they have aged well and acquired complex taste and nose.

I would put on sandals made of used car tires (fifty cents) and an ankle-length local cotton robe, not unlike my grandma's nightgown, without any underwear. I would join the circle every evening. "Bonjour Monsieur Terence! Ça va?" the sages would greet me, with smiles and outstretched arms, since they yearn for listeners. Some would half-rise and point, making a place for me. Monsieur Terence—that is how I am known on Gore. Monsieur Terence is healed by returning to Africa; she calms and at the same time excites my soul.

My other house, in the secret city of Prague, has been renovated—in 1680. It is built of rock, with spacious rooms and ceilings as high as the sky. The walls are massive, two feet thick, and the windows are tall but narrow, to make it quiet and warm. The antique furniture is arrayed so sparsely in the vast spaces that it enhances my feeling of freedom. The paintings and sculptures are a mix of abstract and romantic, pleasing to my eye.

It stands in a narrow lane across from a baroque church where music-lovers (local heathens) congregate. The section of town is called Mala Strana, which means Small Side. The "small" is one thing I especially like about the place. Wherever I wander in the neighborhood, I am taken captive by immovable capsules of history: the mutant gargoyles on roofs, ready to parachute; marble saints with benevolent grins half-eaten by acid rain; sculptured brass doorknobs polished by thousands of calluses; glass windows so old one can see the ripples of the flow of these liquid crystals; cobblestones leveled into the ground by the wheels of coaches of ancient nobles and by paupers' heels. It is known that gold is so precious because its surface does not react chemically with the molecules of gases and fluids—so it always glistens. But the breath of the centuries has misted over the golden mosaics and gold-plated angels in the cathedrals of this, my, town to acquire the warmth of velvet.

Sometimes, just before the sun sets behind the Petrin Hill, all the city seems coated with the golden velvet, too. That is the time when I would don my disguise of an army surplus jacket, workpants, and Czech socialist shoes of plastic (unique in their warning from the manufacturer not to wear them in weather below freezing or above 82° Fahrenheit). I amble up the hill on Neruda Street, past the main gate of the Castle, further up to "U Cernyho Vola"—the "Black Angus" beerhall. And there, with other patrons in similar disguise, under a veil of cigarette smoke and in the vapors of Kozel beer, I engage in dissection, sometimes autopsy, of life, with vehemence and alcohol-induced passion and with the local sarcasm and irony I have learned here. "Ahoj Terence!" someone might greet me. "Terence, vole, come on, sit down here!" A few would pull out chairs for me. The topic of life is inexhaustible, the mysteries many—so I have to go to Prague often, and I do.

When I come to the "Bull's Eye" on Duval street in Key West, even before I reach the bar, I can hear my name. It might come from a table by the stage or one by the window, but most often it comes from the bar, made from the hull of the unfortunate *Panama*, wrecked on Alligator Reef. "Hey, Terence, come here!" Or, "Terence is here. Hey, buddy, here!" And so I bought a house in Key West, in the Florida Keys, remembering Jindra, the adventurer from Papua, with a smile.

My house stands on Olivia Street, near the cemetery, in the old quarter. The street is lined with gambo-limbo trees with the bark shining like the sunburnt ass of a careless tourist. Almost every house has a garden with a banyan tree which sends its roots down from the branches like a parade of crutches, to keep it steady against hurricanes. It is a two-story "wrecker's house" with a widow's walk on the roof from which I can spy the boat traffic on both the emerald expanse of the Gulf and the indigo of the Atlantic (drinking my "papa double" and smoking an illegal Cuban cigar up there, because my local girlfriend convulses at the sight of a cigar in the house).

The walls of the house are massive, two feet thick, coral rock (it is the only "wrecker's house" not built of wood), and the windows are tall but narrow, to keep the rooms cool. The rooms are spacious, with ceilings as high as the sky. The ancient furniture is arrayed so sparsely it leaves open spaces, to enhance my feeling of freedom. The paintings and sculptures are a mix of abstract and romantic, pleasing to my eye.

I spend little time cocooned in the house. I like to be about the town, around people. Mornings are best wasted sitting on the patio of "Croissants de France" on Duval Street. The fruit tarts and chocolate macaroons are as delicious as if baked by Herme, the master frog himself, of "Fauchon" on Place de la Madeleine. The espresso is as pungent and powerful as in downtown Santos. But equally momentous is the tourist crowd gliding by.

South American ladies with painted faces, stumbling on high heels in taut illiberal jeans, buying, buying. Europeans with eyes on everything even vaguely historical, cameras and video-super-8s in hand, in T-shirts without inscriptions or pictures, their brand-new suntans preserved by glistening moisturizers. There are Americans, two hundred pounds each, in "Sloppy Joe's Bar" T-shirts loose over their enormous bellies, shopping, and college kids in factory-torn-and-holed outfits laughing, blessed by ignorance of the passing away (in a couple of years) of their days of true friendship. The local black folks saunter by in perennially good disposition; they are the darkest breed of Bahama negroes—not outbred, still.

And Japanese, who photograph themselves standing at attention in front of every church and bar, with frozen smiles, in that heat. Male gays come in pairs. Key West boasts (along with the highest density of bars per capita in the USA) what might be the highest density of gays per inhabitant. They are at home here. They do not hold hands; they wear clothes from the department store. Some forget to put on their earring. They are at home here.

Not often, a bearded fisherman or lobster-trapper squeezes by, easily recognizable as not belonging any more.

A couple of years ago I had found myself in "Croissants de France" again, in a pleasant chat with French-accented waitresses of handsome face and sympathetic chest. "*Ç'est dommage*"; it's a pity, she had said, when I announced my intention to leave. It was a very good start of a day, and I decided to return. I wandered up Duval, turned right onto Green Street, passing the AIDS Hospice and the Cuban grocery, and right again onto Simonton. There was a new art gallery and antique store there, and I needed an old chair. The owner answered my greeting with an inviting smile, so soon we found ourselves in conversation. He had a foreign accent which turned out to be Dutch.

The anatomy of his face intrigued me. It was carved of ironwood. Sharply outlined masticatory muscles of a laborer bulged on the hard jaw. His strong nose, flanked by good cheekbones, was slightly bent to one side; narrow lips did well in a smile. The features were overlaid by an expression of intelligence, an untough, calm presence; maybe his green eyes did the trick to enthrall me. I recognized a man of great physical might in an instant and observed his naked forearms only to confirm my impression. Indeed, from the elbow to the wrist the cords of muscles were stretched and packed tightly, as in a drawing from an anatomy textbook after removal of the skin.

Soon I was to learn he used to be a member of the Olympic Team of Holland, the country's decathlon champion. His name was Jan Diepering. A decathlon man—the ultimate physical specimen in sports! I was intrigued and, soon, enthused.

In no time, we discovered that our mutually most-venerated man in athletics was the long-distance runner Emil Zatopek, the "Czech Locomotive." Jan locked the door of the shop and put on the sign "CLOSED," the moment he learned that I had visited Zatopek in Prague, seen several of his famously bizarre victories, and read books about him. He gestured with youthful enthusiasm, his physique emanated jaguar-like swiftness, as he paced between the antique chairs recalling memories from Olympic games and memories about the phenomenon Zatopek. His motions had the fluidity and sparseness which comes from restraining one's power and speed. I liked to watch him and loved to talk with him. We reminisced till darkness crept in, agreeing on everything.

I visited him once more, about half a year later, and we continued as if there had been no interruption. I took him to the "Bull's Eye," where some of the patrons knew him too, yet nobody knew about his sporting life. He ordered a nonalcoholic "Shirley Temple," disgusting Eddy, the barman and a friend of mine, and drawing boos from the rowdies by the bar. We had a good time, a famously good time.

Then I traveled to Gore and then to Prague, and more than a year went by before I found myself on Duval Street with my espresso and a view of the passing students on their spring-break rites. I did not linger too long; I was looking forward to seeing my friend, Jan Diepering. The allée of rugged mahoganies on Simonton greeted me with new glossy greens after the recent rain. It had washed the shop window of Jan's enterprise, too.

I entered with an expectant smile, but did not see him. Two men standing behind the office desk stopped talking, and one of them, the taller, answered my greeting. I did not recognize either one. I asked if I could talk to Jan Diepering; when will he be back? The taller of the two men gave me a questioning look, and it took him a while to point at his partner: "Well, here is Mr. Diepering. You go ahead, Sir."

I talked with Jan, with this shriveled man with sunken cheeks and eyes set deep in his skull that did not look at me, a pale cast to his face as if he were under fluorescent lights, his skinny arms motionless along his body. Uneasily we exchanged sentences (I don't recall about what). I apologized for some urgent business I had to attend to and left, confused and feeling embarrassed. In truth I felt like shit. All the way home I wondered how one could decline so much in such a short time. Perhaps he had just recovered from a serious illness, or an operation. What happened to Jan? I'd have to go to see him when he would be alone in the store.

Then I had to leave the city.

My main residence, near Storrs in Connecticut, sits on many acres of an undisturbed mixed forest. It was the early morning of an overcast day in July when I went to the gully to pick mushrooms. Boletuses and chanterelles grow there in summer, and after a rain one can find the delicious purple "horn of plenty" (called "angel of death" by some "experts") in large clumps. This morning's expedition was a fruitful one, and soon I had filled the basket. I sat down on a patch of moss under my favorite maple above the gully. I wondered how might be the weather in Key West, now; how is my garden being overgrown there in the rainy season. How is my friend Jan?

I visualized his face from my last visit with him: the eyes set deep, worry in them and something else I cannot describe, his ears standing out (I had not noticed his ears before), his cheeks pallid and caved—the suggestion of a skull, his hair without luster above the sweaty forehead. Suddenly it came to me—it felt like being hit by a stone to the chest; I had to take a deep breath.

I knew these features; I had seen this likeness in pictures, on television. Those ancient eyes in young men on their deathbeds. Those eyes and hollowed cheeks covered with a pale stretched parchment I recognized. I knew the disease, which my mind had refused to associate with an Olympic athlete. My legs could barely carry me to the house.

In the afternoon on the same day I flew by commercial airline to the Keys—I don't own a jet plane. I ordered a Bloody Mary. The only thing I carried was the basket with mushrooms picked in the gully—for Jan. *I will tell him the truth: Sorry, I did not recognize you the last time, Jan; you looked like hell. Insensitive to say it in such a way, but it will set everything straight.* He will know that I am open with him, that whatever I'll say next will come from my heart, naked. People lie a lot.

How bad all this is! I'll tell him I'm gonna help; money can buy a lot of help, but I will not mention the money. I know people, doctors; experimental drugs might be the way to go, some way to hope. There must be a goddamned hope, for Christ's sake. I'll give him the mushrooms, tell him how to cook them the Japanese way, with soy sauce and sake. To take his mind off things.

I'll tell him about Tetsuo Itoh, how he taught me to cook these mushrooms. How Itoh used to make brass wind instruments and how, during the war, he solved the problem of bending exhaust pipes for Zero fighter planes, bent them like trombones, made millions and then, after the war, he chose to become a cook, a plain cook. I'll tell him the story. Just to take his mind off things. Christ, there must be hope, something to do about that disaster. Maybe I shouldn't tell him how he looks. Yes, I know what I'll do.

I'll enter: "Hey ya, Jan! How's my pal! Hey, so great to see you! I'll slap his back, and I will laugh. Not much, though. That's what I will do when I enter. Maybe."

The plane was going down, and I could see Stock Island and behind it, the outline of the city, the old lighthouse on Whitehead Street, a Navy cruiser in the docks and treetops with curly hairdos suggesting the course of streets. It looked tropically beautiful, but this time the picture went only to my subconsciousness. *Hell, I'll see to it. We'll do something; there must be something to do, some hope.*

A taxi took me to Simonton street. I let the taxi go. I looked for Jan's gallery but got confused. I retraced my steps, as one should when lost, to the Cuban grocery and the AIDS hospice, then walked back—but there just was no gallery on Simonton. It was like a bad dream.

"Yes, my boy, the gallery used to be right here. You are in the right place," the old lady answered my question. She looked amused by my puzzlement. "It has been gone for a month, or so. Here it used to be." She pointed to a vacant lot across the street. I recognized the mahogany tree.

"They wrecked it?"

"Yup, they tore the whole building down. There will be a Winn Dixie store here." She turned her head from side to side and lumbered away. "Another one."

I crossed the street as if in a haze and sat down on a pile of broken cinderblocks, looking at the garbage strewn around, splintered two-by-fours, cigarette butts, plastic bags, crumbled pages of Keynoters and shit. It hurt me bad. "Where are you, Jan? Where are you? My friend, my decathlon man!"

That wailing helped Terence wouldn't surprise experienced mourners. The pain in his chest dulled, a little. He had rarely cried in his life, but there was nobody around. Just this pile of broken cinderblocks, and bricks, a lonely condom, his mushrooms wilting in the heat, the "angels of death" turning black.

Sweat poured from him when he tripped over the rubble. His arms flailed in the air—he almost dropped the basket. On the street he turned south to his house. Maybe, he thought, he could save the boletuses; boletus is such a sturdy fungus. If he freezes it. Maria will know. He could not concentrate his thoughts well.

He crossed the street, waivered, and leaned on the trunk of a mahogany, looking at the sky. The silhouettes of palms were growing darker now, rustling like bones in the nor'easter from the Atlantic, which always blows stronger late afternoon this time of year. Good sailing wind. But it makes one see things disordered, because the brain expands and pushes on the eyeballs.

The Killing of
He-Who-Is-Without-Shadow

From high in the air the village of Eskimo Point resembles a spilled load of cardboard boxes on the deserted shore of the bay. Just mirrors of small lakes decorate the bleak expanse of the surrounding tundra, as far as the horizon. In the black ink of Hudson Bay, quite far off the shore, pods of beluga whales move slowly in synchrony. The Inuit people would wish them closer to the coast at this season of a year, since there is an urgency in gathering enough stocks of meat and blubber for winter. And winter is in the air; one can smell it in the evening.

There is no word to describe the smell of winter in the language of *quabluna*, the white man, or in Inuit. But there are many Inuit names for polar bears, who follow the shore through the village to their southern denning grounds. They come at this time of year. Perhaps, they too smell winter in the air.

The southwestern sky played colors with the orange target suspended above the horizon of Hudson Bay. But still snow geese could be spied in the distance, despite the hour, late by quabluna's watch. Most children dreamt already; some huddled under a blanket from the Hudson Bay Company store, some were heaped under a caribou skin, hugging each other for warmth. The older youngsters, still unmarried, rejoiced in the game of doused lights and other copulation schemes in Young People House. That would seem to be the usual summer evening in Eskimo Point.

But tonight the women intensified their visiting to discuss the eagerly anticipated drawing by the men. This was the most important event of the late summer. Everybody knew that. Women paced from one house to another, crossing their paths at different points between houses, like lemmings, in unpredictable patterns. They shuffled pigeon-toed, wobbling from side to side in the Inuit women's gait; some carried babies in an *amaut*, a pouch under the hood of their caribou parka.

When Akyak met Aklavik, she bent and jerked forward, and the head of little Oolulik popped out at her shoulder, his surprised face surrounded by a halo of wolf's fur lining. Aklavik laughed with approval: "Mmm, mmm, how handsome. Good baby, *namakto*. Eh!"

When women went visiting, their tongues were with them, so Akyak and Aklavik talked some before separating to walk to different houses to talk more. Oh, Akyak almost forgot to mention, that the wife of Sorquaq (Sorquaq and his wife were *Padlermiut*, "caribou people," from the faraway tundra of Padlei. These people knew nothing of seals and beluga. So strange.)—that she, the wife of Sorquaq, has lain overnight with young Napartuk. That will make Napartuk the fourth one, just this summer. How interesting, the women thought.

"Well, her good reputation might spread, and her husband's honor increase. *Uvang okrartunga*; I have spoken." Akyak tried to look serious, in vain.

"Eh, eh, my mother said it is good for a woman to collect memories," Aklavik said. "That later in life a woman will look backward, but not forward, for the thrills of life, she told me, my mother." Both women nodded, and their eyes took on a distant expression, as if looking backward.

"She pinches her cheeks to take a good color, often, often," Akyak giggled.

"Eh, she might not let her hair loose to show she has the period, it is said," Aklavik added, and the women laughed, putting their noses so close they touched. What a pleasure! The wife of Sorquaq laughs with many men. Maybe, this is the way of Padlermiut, it has been deduced.

"Some words are spoken to the air."

"Somebody is thinking of meat."

The women started to walk backwards, still smiling at each other, before turning to their destinations. The wind from the bay raised swirls of dust from the disturbed ground between houses, and women sped up their crossings and pulled hoods over their heads to keep their progeny buried deep in the parkas' amaut. When the sun dove into the bay, all the women of Eskimo Point had already made several pleasurable offerings to the great Spirit of Visiting, with the exception of Tutiak and Ayorsalik.

Ayorsalik had been in trouble; she was shamed by a loss of face. Up until recently, her marriage to two men had worked to the satisfaction of all three involved. She could take care of the soapstone lamps so they never sooted; she dried the *kamiks* well for both husbands; she scraped skins with the *ulu* knife without a single nick; she set and tended many fox traps to get enough skins for cash to buy tobacco; with narwhale sinew she could make stitches so small that seams on her sealskin kamiks and kayak covers were invisible. She was an Eskimo woman, Inuk, to be sure.

She had been rented out to laugh with men of the village by her two husbands, now and then, and that caused much felicity to many, because she was cheerful and quite beautiful. Looking at her face from the side, one could not see her nose at all, so small was it (not protruding like a narwhale horn), and her hare-skin panties were filled very well, without stuffing moss in them. So all men desired her, and some women envied her. A deal had been made, a deal honorable and fair as judged by the villagers and all involved: the income from Ayorsalik's excursions to the igloos of men who rented her would be split into three equal parts for her and for each of her husbands. Since Ayorsalik was no *sequajuq*, lazybones, the income was good, and all three members of the family could smoke enough and buy corn flakes from the H.B.C. store.

However, it became common knowledge, recently, that some of the gains Ayorsalik did not divide by three but only by two. The older of her husbands had been the shorted one, and the only one of the whole village who did not know, as is often the case. This is how Ayorsalik lost face and was dishonored in such a way that she was ashamed to show her face tonight.

The other of the two women who did not participate in visiting was Tutiaq, wife of Minik. Tutiaq, the coveted one. She had become a woman of great consequence, since in her house the men were gathering to draw who would shoot *nanuk*, the polar bear. She was their host, and it will be remembered.

The Canadian Government rations one polar bear *(Ursus maritimus)* per year to be shot by a man of Eskimo Point Village. If it is wounded and escapes, no attempt to shoot another bear can be made that year. The proceeds from the skin, skull, and claws, many thousands of dollars, are to be shared by all the families of the village.

Sometimes it is agreed that the front third of the skin, *nanurak*, can be kept by the shooter, to be made into outer pants.

The last few hunters were still arriving in Tutiaq and Minik's house. Ayagutaq entered. "*Igloo namakto unaktoalu,*" he commented on the warmness of the house and smiled his peculiar smile which everybody admired. His upper lip was split all the way to the nostril due to a congenital harelip which had not been repaired. He sat down near the pot boiling on the gas stove, rolled a cigarette with one hand, lighted it, and blew the blue smoke through his cleft lip in a way which children often requested to observe. The smoke made a sheet that folded into several whirls raising up, which was very beautiful. A renowned storyteller he was, but tonight was no occasion for a story, not even a true one.

"*Aiya! Pollak pak tunga.*" I am visiting, said Ungarpaluq, swaying his parka when he entered, as if to shake off imaginary snow. He was a famed hunter, reputed to have spent two days and one night motionless above *allu*, the breathing hole a seal makes through the ice, before harpooning the seal and taking it out with one pull, in the way of *nanuk*, the polar bear. When he sat down his movements were slow, as if harnessing his might. He stretched his legs and remained calm, as always.

Last came Quapagnuq. (It is certain he had killed two Dene Indians while hunting caribou near Churchill River last year.) "Somebody comes visiting, as it happens." They shook hands with Minik, raising them eyes-high and bending their heads. Quapagnuq sat down, lifted his parka, and scratched his belly. Last fall he had shot a polar bear. With one bullet.

They were all here, now, all twelve hunters of the village confident enough to face the mightiest predator in the world, the only one known to attack a man without hesitation. Nanuk, the eternal wanderer, would meet one of these men, and the man would not show fear and would even deny that a word for retreat can be found in his Inuit language. Even in the secret abyss of his mind a seed of doubt about that had not been allowed to sprout.

In that prefabricated house, shipped in by the government from Churchill, the hunters sat in a circle on the floor of wooden planks. The house had been made Eskimo-cozy by the odor of men, by hanging skins, fur clothing, and fox traps on the walls, and by the steam rising from a large pot. The smell of boiling caribou meat, *tuktuk*, and seal blubber, *muktuk*, added to the well-controlled excitement which showed only in the eyes of the men, not on their weathered, powerful faces. Theirs were the faces of men who have not known chiefs, headmen, or almighty gods. The pieces of muktuk curled, and the hostess, Tutiaq, assessed their tenderness by piercing through them with a stick. Her rosy cheeks and permanent smile revealed her happiness at being able to host this occasion by offering the best to the best.

Then Minik, her husband, rose up and talked with gravity, the way a host and hunter of his great reputation is supposed to talk. "One wishes you can lower yourself to taste the poor carcass this *Inuk-koak*, old man—can offer you." He hung his head down, letting his long hair fall over his face. Not one hair was grey. "It is inedible," he continued, "and you would show me kindness if you'll leave me now with my shame and my useless woman. *Uvanga okrartunga*, I have spoken."

Upon this invitation the men started to eat. The chunk of steaming meat was passed around. Each man bit into it, cut it with a knife in front of his lips, and passed the meat to his neighbor. They smacked their lips and praised this incomparable delicacy. When the succulent *muktuk* made the rounds, they farted politely and belched, to show they were digesting with appreciation.

"*Umm! Mammaraii?*" Delicious; what makes it so good? mumbled Kaviuk, the simple man, his strange face serious, his eyes mere slits, his mouth open. "Ace, ace", he said, as was his habit of saying on many occasions, not only when playing cards, his passion. He could not talk well; "ace" he would say when things were good. And times were good for him often, because the diminished powers of his mind did not allow him to comprehend well the causes of adversities in life. He was not laughed at because he showed abilities to survive the harshness of the arctic, because he understood the hunt, and dogs, and friendship.

Dogs were "aces." While he made dogs with a whip, he made friends with kindness and helping hands, not with wit or speaking, in both of which he possessed only rudiments. He understood stealth in the hunt and the value of a bullet. So he survived, did Kaviuk. "Umm, umm," he said, and licked his lips and wiped the grease off his fingers in his hair.

Nobody else talked; their thoughts were ahead of them, on the drawing for nanuk. When the last piece of meat—of *tuktuk* and of succulent *muktuk*—had disappeared, nobody dozed off, as is the custom sometimes. No story was offered. Tutiaq moved to the corner, trimmed the lamp, and lighted herself that which banishes weariness—a pipe. Then Minik, with calculated carelessness, tossed a can from Dunhill tobacco into the middle of the circle of men. Twelve small bones of equal size from the flippers of a seal rattled in the can, announcing the draw. The men looked at the can, not at each other, wondering, perhaps, about their chances.

Great Ungarpaluq picked up the can: "It will not be just if such a lame and half-blind man would draw the black bone. Nanuk would be safe, and the village sad. So one will draw." He opened the lid and, looking away, he pulled out a white bone. He put the lid on and passed the can to Totterat, clockwise, the direction stories are always told. His hopeful dream came to an end; his face showed no emotion, of course.

Totterat briefly commented on his lack of hunting skills (mostly true), drew a white one too, and passed the can further. And so it went around, all the men drawing white bones, none commenting on his misfortune. One-but-last was Kaviuk. He understood the meaning of this lottery and showed excitement by wheezing and inhaling deeply after each hunter pulled the bone out of the can. He could not manage a speech when opening the can, as others before him had done. He tilted his head far back, staring at the ceiling with an open mouth, when his hand reached into the can and pulled out the seal bone stained black with a mixture of oil and lamp soot.

It lay on his palm while he looked at it. His fingers closed into a tight fist over the bone, so tight his knuckles became white. A strange sound came from him; then he looked around at the other men. "Ace," he whispered.

The men nodded their heads. "*Namakto,*" very good, Minik said after a while and pointed to Kaviuk with an outstretched arm. All the men said "eh, eh, eh," then, and did not reveal their thoughts.

Kaviuk stayed awake that night. He sat on a pile of discarded skins in his shelter, which was not the Government's prefabricated house but a toolshed left in Eskimo Point by a group of astronomers who had come to observe an eclipse of the sun there years ago. He held his 30/30 carabine in one hand; the other still clutched tightly over the black seal bone. It was still predawn, the eastern horizon tinted faintly green above the pink outline of the distant vastness of the tundra, when Kaviuk emerged from his shed in the only caribou parka he owned, sealskin shoes, and kamiks, to step noiselessly over ground hardened by the morning freeze. His carabine was slung on his back horizontally with the rope strap over his chest in the Eskimo way.

His steps were certain, his direction clear, toward a small hill about a mile from the village. He bypassed carefully two large circles of stones, remainders from ancient times at which they had weighted down the skin tents of his forefathers. Near the summit of the hillock he stopped, turned around, and scanned the landscape around the village and along the shore. The flat and barren ground could not conceal the whiteness of a polar bear for miles; there was no snow, yet. The light was sufficient; no *nanuk* in sight.

There were two graves just under the summit of the hill, a favorite place for Kaviuk to sit on summer evenings. Villagers thought he came there to ask for wisdom from his ancestors to improve his feeble mind. Through the stones and broken driftwood he could observe a skull, bones, a deck of cards, the rusted head of an axe, and the shaft of a harpoon. He bent down, looked at the hollow eyes of the skull, and smiled as if meeting a friend. This time he did not sit down but continued to climb the few yards to the top of the hill. The other side of the hill gently sloped down to a small lake. It was covered with a rubble of boulders, dwarf willows not higher than a foot, berry bushes now heavy with fruit, and pillows of moss.

They saw each other at the same instant, and the polar bear, without a moment of hesitation, started toward Kaviuk at a rapid pace. The hunter stood erect and calm. He took his rifle off and cocked it. That was the only moment his eyes left the animal. At fifteen yards the man called: "*Audlar mat!*" "One has arrived!" The bear raised his might up on his hindpaws, walking like a man, showing his enormity, two thousand pounds of power at an awesome height and wrath. *Tara i tualuk:* he-who-is-without-shadow. *Tara i tualuk.*

Kaviuk aimed his carabine, then, and shot him through the heart. He had been told many times that cartridges are expensive, that he must aim calmly. He did not reload, did not move; his weapon remained pointed at the bear. The bear dropped on all fours and charged forward. It collapsed with a moan at the feet of the motionless man, the true Inuk.

That is how the villagers found them. Great Ungaparluq took the rifle from Kaviuk's hands and put it on the ground carefully. Then he slapped Kaviuk's back: "*Namakto, namakto!*" Children came. They romped around, yelling, pointing imaginary guns at the carcass.

Women came. They talked and laughed in groups. Their faces were very happy. They were deciding, perhaps, which of them would visit the shed tonight. The toolshed left by *quabluna* astronomers.

Then the men of the village came. Some slapped their thighs; some checked the fur and teeth of the nanuk. They all slapped Kaviuk's back, one by one. All of them.

What I Will Do !

Frau Chermak, alias Marus Cermakova, arrived twenty minutes late at the embassy party. Her beautician in the Hotel Intercontinental, the poshest establishment in Prague, had confused appointments, causing Frau Chermak the late arrival and losing her as a client forever. Frau Chermak was still fuming when she parked her BMW 318 on Pevnostni Street in the Swiss Embassy parking space. She threw a shawl of Thai silk over her shoulders, adjusted the hat on her beehive hairdo, and lifted her A-frame from the seat, with some effort.

Her hat had a sprawling rim on the left side and a narrow one on the right, which was lifted and attached, giving the thing a semblance of an Australian bush hat. However, the two little birds constructed from real imported feathers, decorating its south side, and the flair and proportions of the design, differentiated it from a hat for adventures in the bush. Nevertheless, she felt adventurous, and nervous, too, in anticipation of the opinions of Frau Müller, Frau Novack, and that cow Poznerova. They would lie to her, anyway.

By the entrance, she almost collided with that cow Poznerova, who had parked her Mercedes right across from the entrance to the embassy just to remind everybody who owned the silver automobile. Poznerova was coming late intentionally, that's for sure, so she could apologize loudly that her reason for being late was an important social affair she had to attend with her industrialist hubby. Marus Cermakova, introducing herself as Frau Chermak now, had no chance to match that, a fat zero of a chance. Because her husband, Pepa, was a goddamned loser. That was the reason.

Pepa (Josef) Cermak, originally from the Branik quarter of Prague, was not a loser, really. He was just a dreamer. Pepa was a pure dreamer, not one of those who have a dream and strive to realize it, but one of those genuine dreamers whose visions remain in the realm of fantasy.

Rare fortunes in his life, sometimes, made it look as if his reveries had been forged into reality by Pepa's willpower and skills. But a closer examination of events would have revealed that, indeed, these were accidents, events of serendipity.

Let us take, for instance, his marriage to Marus, Frau Chermak, which, as of today, had happened a quarter of a century ago. Theirs was not a stormy, sweeping love affair. True, Pepa liked her okay, and he was impressed when she made him Wienerschnitzel and bought the right beer to go with it, all by herself, and when she took it upon herself to decide which movie to see, what to do for the weekend, and what Pepa should wear. But most of all he liked her ample behind—he loved it.

Because he was a dreamer, he often dreamt about that part of her anatomy in situations of lovemaking. But, as usual, most of his dreams remained in dreamland, since the attitude of Marus toward matters of sex bordered on indifference, big butt or not. She became pregnant anyway, and it is a matter of record that she refused any of the available alternatives to marriage, such as the suggested interruption. The day when Pepa informed them in detail about his predicament and Marus's menstrual history is remembered well by all members of his KKK soccer team (Kosire Kangaroo Killers).

Their game with Sparta Team C was in halftime when the telephone rang in the locker room. All of Pepa's teammates had wished her menses would recur, and their hearts sank with the expected ringing of the phone. Pepa, long-faced, bravely took the receiver, listened, lifted his eyes to the ceiling, and hung up. The locker room was totally devoid of sound. "Did not come," Pepa announced; he sat down and looked demurely at the floor. The desired periodic menstruation had not yet come, and there was no realistic hope for it to arrive after this critically late date. A few eyes of the tough and seasoned soccer warriors appeared glossy; the goalie, Mita Berchtold, and the left forward, Jirka Sour, mumbled a few words of sympathy.

The civil wedding ceremony took place in late July 1968. All went well; everybody got drunk and happy. This was a special time of great happiness for the nation, with the Prague Spring of Freedom, and victories over the rule of communist achievers and Soviet oppression. Marus and Pepa departed for their honeymoon on their Cezeta scooter, with a tent and a supply of canned food, to the coast of Yugoslavia. In the campground near Split they learned from their portable radio that their country was being occupied by Soviet troops and that Russian tanks were so thick in Prague one hesitated to cross the street.

The instant rumor in tent-camp was that Czechoslovakia would become a new Soviet republic. The question of emigration, of not returning home, came up with urgency in circles formed around the kerosene camp stoves and solid-fuel burners. Pepa was against it because, as he argued, he loved his mother, his soccer team was in a winning streak, and in his vocabulary the word emigration had never existed. Marus, now at the beginning of the second trimester of her pregnancy, solved the situation by announcing that she would not deliver no kid in no Soviet republic for no disgusting Bolsheviks.

Since there were many Czech families and couples on the coast of the Adriatic Sea, the ground for happy campers turned into a nervous refugee camp. Soon, one by one, the campers departed and spread all over the civilized parts of Europe. With presentable suntans and a collection of seashells, Pepa and Marus left the camp for Switzerland, the country with the highest standard of living, as they had learned in the newspaper. Looking at their possessions piled up on the back rack of the scooter, it seemed urgently desirable to improve their standard of living. So they became foreigners.

The Swiss kindness to foreign nationals was incomprehensible to Pepa and Marus. Everything was alien to them. Some Swiss customs were difficult to get used to; some puzzled them for many years to come. One source of wonder was the religious beliefs of the Swiss, because neither Pepa nor his Catholic bride had ever known anybody in their old country who truly believed in supernatural beings, such as God or other gods. Marus believed in a high standard in possessions—and was determined to achieve it, even if it would take hard work by Pepa.

In the winter of their emigration year their little skinhead, Pepa the 2nd, was born. Marus hung a picture of two chubby angels above his cradle. Under their spread wings was an inscription: "On March 15th our Pepa II opened his blue eyes to illuminate brightly the gray days of our life." Pepa the 2nd did that, occasionally, but he was a dreamer like his dad. So the day he reached legal adulthood, he departed for America to fulfill his American dream, to wash dishes in a "Chart House" restaurant in the Rocky Mountains of Aspen,

Colorado. He promised to keep in touch on condition that his parents would never offer any advice to him, anymore.

After years and then two long decades had passed in relative prosperity and health, middle age arrived, and Pepa found himself in avoidance of mirrors. Much of his hair went down the drain, and his pouchy belly seemed to resist the tightening of his belt. The distribution of fat deposits on Marus would surprise a student of anatomy, but would fail to please him. While causing bodily harm, the passing of time also changed the ways they saw things, the logic of their judgment, and the way they communicated with each other. Their mutual verbal and physical contacts decreased.

They still held onto a few traditions, but those traditions became tired through repetition and over time. Love was still performed every Wednesday, but now with doused lights. A barbecue or cheese fondu was still held once a month, but now with acquaintances instead of with friends. The scooter which had brought them to their new homeland (on which Marus used to sit behind Pepa holding onto his waist and flattening her breasts against his back) was replaced by a tiny Fiat 500 (where Marus sat touching her knees with Pepa's), which was later replaced by a more respectable Opel (where Marus sat far beyond touching distance). Thus their automotive progress had followed the pattern of a reverse relationship between economic well-being and the warmness of human relations.

They had rented an apartment with a spacious balcony near the park and had furnished it with copies of antique furniture, authentic down to the hand-drilled woodworm holes. Marus had acquired a fur coat made of the pelts of unborn fetuses of black Persian sheep, and a ring with a three-quarter karat Colombian emerald. Pepa had a Schaffhousen watch and a golden neckchain the thickness of those worn by professional tennis players. He remained interested in soccer but had developed a new passionate interest in professional cycling.

Eddy Merckx became his all-time hero, and Pepa could recite the years of his five victories in the Tour de France and five in the Giro d'Italia. He went to see him demolish the peloton in the Vuelta á España. Pepa saw how "Le Cannibal" ate them all alive and related it, over and over. And then there was the topic of Fausto Copi, the skeletal genius, whose body seemed to be just an appendage to his enormous legs, with Copi's greenish face a copy of Tutankhamen's mummy. Disputes with Pepa's colleague Luigi were endless, and the question of how would the divine Fausto compare with "Le Cannibal," if he were alive today, had never been resolved, to the delight of both fans. Pepa had to suffer for his hobby, since in the eyes of Marus it was a useless pursuit compared to the hobby of their neighbor Franz, cabinetmaking, or of Dietrich upstairs, who was an accomplished cook. Pepa did not even ride the bicycle himself.

For their vacations, they always settled on Majorca, the island with the mightiest dracena tree in the world and the densest concentration of vacationing grocers and shopkeepers in Europe. On their last vacation there, Marus and Pepa had discovered large groups of Czech tourists. From what they learned from the tourists, their country, Czechoslovakia, had been liberated, communism abolished, the borders opened wide, and everybody had hurried abroad to breathe deeply the vanilla-sweet scent of freedom. Back in Switzerland, all Czechoslovaks talked about nothing else than the new politics, and one by one they traveled to visit the old country. Most visited for the first time in over two decades of living the lives of foreigners in the cleanest and most orderly country of the Switzers. They longed to wander through the ancient, worn alleys of old Prague, cozy with dog-droppings and overturned trash cans.

Like Pepa, they dreamt about smoke-filled beerhalls and beerholes, like *"U krvavýho drápu,"* where the "Kozel" beer is always eight degrees centigrade and the tablecloth is stained with beer-foam and with mustard from steaming sausages, where old boys put a hand over your shoulder even before they get drunk, and strangers argue politics, complaining about everything, and then sing songs they learned in the army, and their women sit there too, with nipples visible through their blouses, drinking beer with beer-bellied guys with bulbous noses, laughing at their disgusting jokes, and then telling intimate secrets to passers-by, while other women push their stumbling mates through the door homeward, and the waiter spills the beer, carrying four mugs in each hand, and then separates those who halfheartedly raise their fists to settle the question of cheating by their soccer team, be it AC Sparta or SK Slavie or Bohemians, and all, eventually, meet through the night, hearts filled with freedom, pissing in the asphalt painted pissoir with the stench so bad and sweetly memorable, like no other in the world.

Pepa and Marus drove to Prague the next summer. Pepa's dreams were fulfilled in every detail, in many a suspicious beer establishment, and Marus enjoyed herself, too. Her Italian shoes were admired by her high school mates; her linen sweater elicited envious looks at Wenceslas Square, and her cousin freaked out about the emerald. It was not easy to come back to the cold majesty of the autumnal Alps.

They had returned to Switzerland at the beginning of September. The nights were getting cold, and something had gone wrong with the complex mechanism lifting and closing the glass walls of the indoor/outdoor swimming pool of Herr Rothweiler. The first day when Pepa returned to work, his supervisor, Herr Vogl, had looked relieved and told him that Rothweiler's problem should be no match for his skills, an easy job. And that he should be on the job tomorrow, as early as first light.

The residence of Herr Rothweiler on the Spiegelsee was regarded even by the rich of the valley as far out, as above their heads with riches, somewhat shameful in its dimensions, perhaps. For the less affluent inhabitants, it was a place to drive by and admire with onomatopoeic sounds, a place shrouded by gossip, sort of a landmark monument to big bucks, i.e., big dreams. Pepa was curious and looked forward to getting there. Marus had already rehearsed her speech to be given to acquaintances about her familiarity with Rothweiler's place. She woke up with Pepa at five, not to prepare him breakfast (she had given up that slavery years ago) but to remind him to remember everything, not to be stupid by paying attention only to some ball-bearings and pulleys. As always, Pepa said: "Sure," and started his Opel.

After a short exchange on the intercom the gigantic gate slid aside, and Pepa drove between rows of palms and flowering exotica in immense containers. Near the entrance to the house he was stopped and waved to a side path by a young man in a suit and tie. The man motioned him to park and to follow him on foot to the swimming pool with the problem. It took about twenty minutes for the limber fingers and technical eyes of the old pro Pepa to have the glass wall moving up and down by touching a few connections in the programming box. A mouse must have bit through one of the wires. The job was done by the time the first rays of the sun touched the smooth surface of the pool. Pepa lit his morning cigarette with a feeling of satisfaction. He inspected, again with admiration, the lifting mechanism and the glass wall of the pool. The castle-like dwelling attached to the pool seemed to him too immense and unreal to get excited about.

The young man with the glacial look and the tie materialized from nowhere. "Mister, Herr Rothweiler would like to talk to you. Follow me, please." He looked at Pepa's cigarette with a stare which almost extinguished it. Pepa did that and followed.

"Why would he like to talk to me? Do you know?" Pepa asked, but received no answer. They went in through the side entrance, crossed several corridors, ascended a narrow staircase, and walked into a room with walls covered with uncracked books that looked as if they had never been touched by human hands. There were tables with globes on them and dark leather sofas that looked never-used, with directional lighting positioned above them that created only a twilight. The young man disappeared without a word. Pepa stood there.

"*So, Sie sind Herr Chermak!*" Pepa almost jumped. Behind him stood a bulky, short man with an agreeable smile, in a black bathrobe and slippers, his hair (what was left of it) still wet. "Rothweiler," he said, and extended his hand. Pepa felt the rings; it was a metal grip, but not an aggressive one. They shook hands.

"*Jawohl. Ja, Ich bin Chermak,*" Pepa recovered. "*Gutten Morgen.*" Rothweiler motioned him through a Gothic door into a smaller semilunar room with a round marble-topped table in the middle of chairs covered with olive green leather. There was an alcove with a classical statue of a nymph-like creature in Carrara marble. In one corner there was a fern tree, in another what looked like a Ming dynasty vase of gigantic dimensions. A silk Persian Isfahan carpet with an elephant-foot design covered part of the floor of painted tiles, and on the only windowless wall hung an abstract painting in a golden frame—it could have been by Léger. This was a nightmare of a room for any interior decorator worthy of his or her profession. But the antique stained-glass windows allowed in only beams of light with properties so miraculous they actually succeeded in creating an atmosphere of warmth and some intimacy.

"You wouldn't mind to have a small breakfast with me, Chermak?" Rothweiler sank into one of the chairs and motioned Pepa to sit down, as if he had already agreed. Then he rang a bell, as one sees in movies about haunted castles, and indeed, an older butler in a dark suit appeared, took a look, and vanished without receiving orders. Rothweiler watched Pepa's wide eyes with an expression of satisfaction.

Rothweiler had a ruddy face and a fleshy nose, seasoned to the color of cabernet, with fine twisting purple lines. His bushy eyebrows contrasted with the sparseness of the hair on his head. His eyes seemed full of energy, despite the sizeable bags under them and the skin-folds covering their outer corners. A triple chin added the joviality expected of multiple chins, but the thickness of the lips could make one suspicious of his smile. He leaned back with ease, in contrast to Pepa's posture.

"Relax, Chermak. Relax yourself!" he said. "We'll have something to bite into. This is a good time, this early morning."

Pepa nodded. "Very nice place, Herr Rothweiler."

"Isn't it? But tell me, you must be Czech with a name like that of yours. Chermak." He leaned forward. "It should be Č-e-r-m-á-k, with a háček above the C and a čárka above the a, long a. Shouldn't it be?"

"Yes, you are right. We came in 1968. From Prague."

"From Praha? Which quarter of Praha?"

"Well, it is called Branik, Herr Rothweiler."

"Branik, Branik, I'll be damned!" Rothweiler beamed. "I used to go swimming there, spent all summers in the Yellow Spa on the Vltava River there," he said. "Wouldn't you know." He looked at the ceiling, and his eyes narrowed to help sharpen his memory. "There was the Blue Spa next to it. Yes, downstream. Is it still there?"

"When we left it was still there, both spas. I used to go to Yellow too, Herr Rothweiler." Pepa cheered up a little.

"You know, I almost drowned there once," Rothweiler continued. "Dove into the water, lost direction, and swam under that floating wooden platform. Do they still have those platforms there?" he asked himself, more than asking Pepa, who looked astonished. Then he learned the story of Herr Rothweiler, whose original name (never revealed) had been changed soon after the communists took over and he had escaped to Switzerland. That was forty years ago.

Pepa heard about his business, importing furniture to starving England from starving postwar Europe and then exporting back the antique furniture from England to still-prosperous Switzerland. Pepa was told, in sketchy detail, of how Rothweiler's millions were made. And he was instructed that the most satisfying fortune is that which is made with the least effort. Then they switched from Hochdeutsch to Czech, his as rusty as Rothweiler's was. The butler brought smoked salmon, poached eggs, then champagne and strawberries ("bubbly— good for your corpuscles"), and espresso, and Cuban cigars. Pepa was careful not to inhale, and managed. By then they were buried in their easy chairs under a blue haze of Cuban smoke.

Rothweiler deposited the ash from his cigar onto remnants of his strawberries and looked at Pepa with a winning smile. He raised the cigar in the air, and his outstretched arm covered the room in the sweeping motion of an orchestra director. "Not bad. Not bad for a refugee!"

All the way to the factory, "not bad for a refugee" resonated in Pepa's head. Rothweiler, calling himself a refugee? Pepa knew he himself could never light a cigar and say that with a winning smile. He could not ever say it because he lived in an apartment and did not even own a Mercedes, forget about a Rolls Royce. He thought about that all day.

At home that evening Marus was strict with him because he did not remember enough about Rothweiler's residence; she gave him a short speech about his uselessness. Now she would have to make up things to tell the neighbors about the good old friend of her husband, the multimillionaire from Spiegelsee. When Pepa closed his eyes in bed, his mind did not go to sleep but generated a great new dream about the future of Pepa Chermak. Great Dream.

As the days passed after the job in the mansion on Spiegelsee, Pepa's plans took a clearer form. They became a daydream, and as such could be directed, like a movie: manipulated and fine-tuned. Pepa, who in the past had notoriously kept his dreams imprisoned in dreamland and prevented them from affecting his reality, this time let the dream escape the confinement of never-never land. He was bloody serious. He'd had it, he had had enough. He'd do it.

May arrived in a hurry, and not only on the calendar. Snow covering the Alpine peaks reflected the sun like a coating of diamonds. The rainbow colors of the meadows buzzed with sounds of bees and crickets and smelled heavenly of spring. Groups of hikers set out on the trails with picnic supplies in their colorful backpacks, laughing. Old folks sat in their gardens, next to plaster dwarfs and trolls, sipping wine, grateful to Nature and to physicians for another year. Switzerland was as beautiful and uncrowded as the limits of European reality would allow.

Pepa came to the factory earlier than usual, made his cup of coffee, took a blank A-1 format paper, and affixed it on his drawing board by taping over the corners. With a marker he wrote on the top: WHAT I WILL DO! He took another sip of coffee, extinguished his cigarette, and in neat script revealed his future, conceived in dreams.

WHAT I WILL DO!

1) Save more money (20,000)
2) Buy me a beamer (BMW 318)
3) Divorce
4) Move back to Prague (Branik)
5) Get me a young and slim one (98–58–88 cm)

He looked at the list in deep thought, not noticing Herr Vogl, the supervisor, standing behind him. "Well, what might this be, Herr Chermak?" Pepa lifted his shoulders and eyebrows, took the list off the board, folded it, and put it in the breast pocket of his jacket. There was a project to be finished by the end of the day, and so he got to it with regained concentration. It was a hard day, but all went well, and Herr Vogel complimented Pepa for his technical imagination.

Back at home, Pepa threw his jacket on the sofa, got a Pilsner Urquell from the fridge, and sank into the easy chair, bushed. Marus told him that he was more fun than a barrel of monkeys, and took his jacket to hang it in the closet. Seeing a folded paper sticking out of the breast pocket, she unfolded it and read: WHAT I WILL DO!

At the same time that Frau Chermak, alias Marus Cermakova, arrived at the party given by the Swiss Embassy in Prague in her BMW 318, Pepa Cermak was just returning home in a crowded tram to their newly acquired mini-apartment, late from his second job, ordered by his wife Marus. Since their re-immigration from Switzerland to the Branik quarter of Prague, all his dreams, including those about evenings in a cozy pub like "*U krvavýho drápu*," had remained unfulfilled. Marus had taken care of his dreams with her aging but iron hand, reminding him, periodically, of his infamous list: "WHAT I WILL DO!"

He asked himself often now: *what shall I do?* And he could not find an answer. Just could not figure out the answer. But there was this letter from junior, from Pepa II. It had come yesterday, all the way from Aspen, Colorado, and on it stamps with Elvis Presley and a bald-headed eagle.

The kid had moved out of the town of Aspen, just a few minutes away in his four-wheel-drive Jeep. He said that the tourists were gone by now, so he was working part-time, evenings, as a waiter and during the day fixing ski tows and lifts. He said they were looking for a skilled mechanic, an experienced hand who could solve problems and work hard. He said that after work they would sit on the porch of their cabin, friends would stop by, they would drink beer, and his pal, Bruce, would play guitar. In the evening, after a sunny day, the air smelled of pine resin, and they could hear buck elks calling from the mountain. And every day, now, they would see a big American eagle gliding through the valley. Like the one on the postage stamp, its wings don't move at all. He said, they are looking for a skilled mechanic, an experienced hand, he said.

And Then There Were None

The animal was dying. They both knew it, and knew better than to talk about it. Olaf had gotten the monkey in the bazaar in Nairobi, the one by the mosque. He had gone there for a new frying pan and instead bought the baby black-faced vervet. It was compressed into a bird cage so small that the tiny monkey had to crouch like a neolithic mummy with her head bent forward and her knees under her chin. Olaf had bargained, but only halfheartedly; so, finally, he had paid almost half the asking price. Lua boy, the seller, who must have known that the monkey was sick, did not even try to conceal his exuberance over this victory over a *mzungu*, white man.

Like a tender bundle of breathing matter she lay limply on a blanket that Olaf and Derek arranged as a nest in a corner of the main room. She did not touch the bananas and refused warmed milk with the passivity of a sick child. Her teary, questioning eyes became even sadder than the eyes of a healthy monkey. Olaf told Derek about saving her from the market, about his trip home in *matatu*, where he almost got into a fight with some idiot who tried to poke her through the cage.

He made Turkish coffee for the both of them, and they sat on the floor watching the animal watching them with those eyes that rarely blinked, revealing little and making one wonder about the sadness of evolution. Sudden sounds and movements frightened her into jerky motions, so they tiptoed to their bedrooms and said goodnight in whispers. A few minutes later they surprised each other sneaking into the main room at the same moment. "Just checking."

Olaf was a Peace Corps volunteer assigned to teach English and biology in Kenya for two years. Many of his peers envied his assignment in Thika. It was a short agony-ride by bus or torture-ride by *matatu* from downtown Nairobi—but still it was out in the country, past the suburbs. Thompson gazelles could be seen near the town at any time and stories abounded of encounters with more exciting wildlife in backyards. It was an East African countryside of surprising exotic sounds, smells, and weather.

Most fortunate was the deal with housing. Olaf's house (not a shack—it had electricity) was a simple structure right at the edge of the school's exercise field or playground. It came with a garden plot made tropically exciting by clumps of banana plants, some cassava, bitter leaves, and a few sugar canes. For shade and for an oversupply of delicious fruit, a dark mango tree leaned on the short wall of the house. It also sheltered a lot of wild creatures: birds, lizards, and also insects for night music. The only disadvantage was that the stones and sticks thrown at the ripe mangoes by local kids and rowdies would fall on the roof and drive Olaf to distraction.

Olaf had planted two rows of tomatoes. The poor soil and rich sun in collaboration had created a delicacy of taste unknown in the produce departments of the shopping centers of America. He had also built a bench of stone-hard *mbutu* wood by the back wall of the house, so he could sit there in the evening and watch the sun setting behind his own banana grove. In the dry season the dust in the air, brought by the Saharian *harmatan*, made the sun grow to enormous dimensions before it descended into the Rift Valley to sleep.

Sometimes Timothy stopped by, and they would share the bench, a few Tusker beers, and memories of the day, until the night-biting mosquitoes threatened them with blackwater fever and chased them inside. Timothy, a local Kikuyu, was also a teacher, always in good cheer with a supply of opinions and stories that were sometimes interesting, and frequently repeated with variations on the ending. He was a good friend, who came by unannounced and often, as all good friends everywhere must do.

Olaf had met Derek in Nairobi in "The Thorn Tree" cafe in front of the New Stanley Hotel. The place was popular mostly with college-aged travelers, who came singly or in pairs, in cotton shirts made in India, jeans, or shorts, the girls with hair braided the Kenyan way (it hurts like hell for days), some with toes and palms painted with henna, and always in sandals, counting shillings carefully before ordering a cheap and barely edible sandwich. One rarely encountered tourists there, in their "white hunter" safari outfits with videocameras over their shoulders, snakeproof boots, and the determined look of Ernest (Hemingway) or Beryl (Markham, of course). With their self-delusions of alluring Africa, the tourists kept to cafes in the Hilton or the Serena, or better yet the Norfolk Hotel.

People would come to the Thorn Tree (pretending thirst, hunger, or such) to see who was passing through town. Guys would check out their chances of meeting a lonely female traveler looking for "advice" or housing. They all read the messages on the bulletin board, nailed right onto the famous thorn tree in the middle of the cafeteria. Some of the messages seemed to have been written by an altogether too happy but shaky hand influenced by the potency of cannabis from Machakos. (Ganja from Mombasa would not have allowed a smoker to write a message at all.)

Olaf had read, "Larry is looking for Sandra, or Sally, McCulough or McCalla, who might be coming from Malindi or Lamu. I love you!!! Call: 23564." Olaf had laughed.

"What's so funny?" Derek had asked, and introduced himself. Olaf had ordered a can of Tusker beer, and a passion-fruit juice for Derek, and they had talked: some football, some baseball, some Kenya. Then they had gone to the "Trattoria" at the corner of Kuanda Street, had eaten Italian, and at the closing hour Olaf had rented his spare bedroom to Derek for six hundred shillings per month, which was worth about forty bucks and satisfied them both. Derek had moved in the next morning and praised the set-up; he liked everything about it.

Olaf's house had one major room. To call it a living room would be inaccurate, since most of the living was done in the bedroom or in the garden. On opposite sides of it were bedrooms, with one window each. The "kitchen" was outside the house under a sheet of corrugated iron supported by four posts, and its equipment was positively native. The outhouse was a sad story for the feeblehearted, which will remain untold. Next to the kitchen was a showerhead attached to the wall of the house in a bamboo enclosure built by Olaf himself—his proud achievement.

Bamboo is a romantic material. Olaf had delighted in watching the color of it change over time from shiny green to green with thin yellow streaks, then to yellow with green streaks, then to solid old gold. He had photographed the same segment of the bamboo enclosure every two weeks, for the record, sprinkling it with water for a glossy effect. He had grown to honor the abode as his home.

Derek had moved two Samsonite suitcases into the vacant bedroom and set up camp there. He was a traveling man who lived out of suitcases, literally, so he had opened the luggage and kept it open by the wall. It never crossed his mind to build or buy a stool or shelves or anything that couldn't be carried out and around. He wouldn't even venerate his cot with a sheet and pillow but slept on it in his lightweight sleeping bag or, during the hot nights of the dry season, on the sleeping bag. When he would leave on trips, his room looked barren and virginally cold even in the passionate tropical heat.

The monkey was never given a name because it faded away too fast. To name her would have made the inevitable only more difficult to bear. The little thing diminished day by day and then, one morning, they found her in the blanket nest, rigid, with one hand over her forehead, eyes closed. Olaf took care of her, digging a tiny grave in the corner of the garden and burying her in a shoebox too big for her body, which had been shrinking since he brought her home.

Derek did not have to go to Nairobi that day and secluded himself in his room until noon. When he came out, he did not talk, and averted his eyes when Olaf talked to him. He refused lunch and looked downcast. There seemed to be an agitation in his gloom. Perhaps he had loved that tiny monkey. She shouldn't have done it to him.

The Second Monkey

Derek was a strange bird, Olaf thought. Actually, the image of a shark (as unlikely as that might sound) had come to Olaf when he'd first met him in the Thorn Tree. It was his teeth, a full mouth of them, that had invoked the likeness of that predator. Derek used to grind his teeth while sleeping, and so it happened that he had worn them down so deeply that all of the teeth had to be capped. The prosthodontist, obviously, had chosen the sizes of his crowns with an unusual megalomania. While this oversized dentition harmonized with Derek's hollow cheeks and with his drawn expression, his eyes were mild, without harshness, and one wondered whether they revealed sadness or kindness.

Besides his physiognomy, his psychology appeared also to be peculiar. He believed in many things. He believed in the National Rifle Association, in the existence of gods, specifically the Christian one, and in abstinences of all kinds. He believed that when a spermatozoon penetrates the zona pellucida of an egg, the resulting cell is a human being. He believed that all men are created equal, with the exception of some of his Kikuyu advisees. He simply believed a lot, by Olaf's standards. He also regarded smokers as despicable, so Olaf had to sneak his occasional joint of cannabis out to the garden and hide with it behind the bananas—"hide in my own goddamn garden!"

Derek would never talk about girls and dating, except once when he described the rendezvous from an ad he'd placed in the newspaper. His date had a nose of such dimensions and curvature that when he saw her waiting for him, he'd actually run away at least a mile, before he felt safe.

"Did you get another date from that ad?"

"Yeah, I got one more. But I did not like her much. I went out with her for a year."

"You did not like her . . . for a year?" Olaf asked.

"Didn't. She always wanted to talk. And to pretend things."

"Pretend things?"

"You know—things." Derek looked to the ground. "Forget it! She was a pain. For Christmas I bought her suppositories for hemorrhoids." Derek gave a humorless laugh.

"What?!"

"Anyway, at the end I sort of started to like her, you know." He revealed his shark dentition. "Then—so you know—she left me. Just like that." Derek looked victorious, I-told-you-so. "Just like that." He snapped his fingers.

Nothing could be said safely, Olaf thought, but the silence embarrassed him after a while. "How about friends, Derek? Do you have some friends at home?"

"I had a friend once, ya. In elementary school I used to have one. Chuck."

Olaf would have liked to talk about friendship but knew that Derek would not comply, because he could not. Neither as a contributor nor as a listener. They had agreed, silently, not to have any more confessional discussions, and Olaf thought it healthier that way.

Derek did not read; he liked to sleep or daydream. But he volunteered to do dishes and the cooking once in a while: spaghetti with Olaf's tomatoes, garlic, olive oil, and Parmesan, when that was available in the Indian *duka* near Jaimia Mosque, which they liked for its owner, a turbaned Sikh of eternal and loud pessimism. Somehow, this basic meal could be eaten often, like bread, and that is what they did.

Derek also took special pleasure in cleaning his double-barreled shotgun (kept illegally, which worried Olaf, his landlord). Weekly, Derek took it apart, oiled it, and aimed it at various objects in the room. His nervous hands would suddenly steady, the finger pulling the trigger in deliberately slow motion. He was proud of the gun, claiming it had historical value; it must have been used by colonial Brits in the good old times during the Mau Mau uprising in romantic Kenya. Olaf did not like the gun and did not like Derek's reasons for liking it. Derek had bought it in Busia, a town near the Ugandan border where he had supervised a "development project" funded by the Rockefeller Foundation, a building demonstration of houses made solely from materials available locally, i.e. mud. "Damn it, you wouldn't believe the waste of money. Just waste," was the sum total of what he would tender about his project, which he called "their project."

As time went by, safe topics for discussion between Derek and Olaf became exhausted, and while tension had been avoided in their mostly mute cohabitation, they had failed to develop what could be called a stimulating relationship. That changed with the arrival of the second monkey. She was a female vervet, again, and Olaf named her Lika. It rhymed with Thika, and she did lick her lips before and after a treat, like a kid. She was the equivalent of a human teenager in both her relative age and her nuttiness; her great hobby was people. For the first few days Derek either avoided her or tried to show indifference to her friendly overtures.

"Derek, she likes you. Lika!" Olaf attempted to help when she sneaked behind Derek and tried to touch his hair.

"So get her away!"

And so it went. After a week, Olaf decided to have a talk about the situation. Derek admitted (with some evasiveness and torturous verbalizing) that he had a problem—because of the first monkey's death. He had liked her a lot, and when she died he resolved not to get attached again to another pet. He switched to simple words with a frankness which surprised Olaf.

"How about if I grow to like this stupid Lika, you know? Like really like her.... And then she would die." Pain showed on his young-old face so clearly that Olaf felt sudden embarrassment for him, got up, and brought in a couple of Tuskers.

"*Barindi. Kuna mzungu!*" He offered it "cold, to a white man," in Swahili, but the front Derek had put up did not relax.

"I don't want to go through that again. It has always been like that with me, you know. You love somebody—and then ... oh fuck it." He reached for the beer, looking away from Olaf. "Well, thanks for the beer, anyway." They did not talk about the monkey any more.

Later that evening Timothy stopped by and, for Olaf, seeing the permanent smile on his wide Kikuyu face felt like sunshine after a cold spell. They took Lika outside and sat on the bench, using the hurricane lamp instead of the moon. Bats were in full acrobatic action, fireflies blinked madly among the bananas, and a cooling breeze began its descent from the Ngong Hills. Derek let Lika creep up and settle on his shoulder for the first time. Timothy mused about the likeness between Derek and the monkey, and then talked about old times, about the uprising and who in town was on which side. Olaf played Springsteen on the tape deck and served beer.

When enough had been consumed, he recited for them his "small" poem he called "Just a Little Piece of Shit to Remember Nights Like This":

> Southern Cross sky,
> equator walking distance.
> Bruce Springsteen on my tape:
> "Born in the USA"
>
> Ngong Hills in moonlit gowns,
> my frangipani-scented night.
> Beware of lions roaming near:
> "Born Free"

When Timothy had left, under stars so bright they lighted his way even without their lunar companion, when Olaf had said goodnight and disappeared into his bedroom for a secret joint of Machakos grass, Derek sat with Lika, alone. He looked into her eyes, for a long time, to the shrill of cicadas from their mango tree.

In the following weeks Derek took over the care of Lika, feeding her, cleaning up after her; he even bought a brush to groom her. They both enjoyed that, she with almost a smile on her face. He always brought her treats from his trips and explained to her where they came from: star fruit from Naivasha, guanabana from Nakuru market, passion fruit from Mombasa. When Olaf was not around, Derek talked to her, mostly about himself. When they were together with Lika his intensity vanished, and his face acquired an appearance of kindness, so skillfully concealed, otherwise. And Lika adored him, in her boisterous, simian way.

Lika was confined to the house most of the time. She was allowed into the garden only under the guarding eye of Derek or Olaf. From the window, Lika loved to watch the students playing. She was fascinated by children; perhaps she couldn't decide if they were monkeys too, because of their size and behavior.

On Friday Olaf's classes finished early. He was working in the garden when Timothy rushed in, all excited, with Lika in his arms.

"She must have got away, the little devil. It could have been her end!" He talked fast, his eyes bulging. "I came to the playground just in time. The stupid kids were throwing stones at her; they tried to encircle her."

"Timothy! Jesus! Is she hurt?"

They inspected her—couldn't find a scratch. She looked frightened, that was all. They would not tell Derek. They had not noticed that the lower right corner of the mosquito screen on the living room window was detached and could be pushed out.

She escaped a second time while Derek was writing letters in his bedroom and Olaf was at school. She approached a crowd of children running around the field with a ball. This time the boys were alert and managed to encircle her. They closed the circle tightly. She screamed and wailed. The boys showed off to the girls how fast they were, how precisely they could aim their stony projectiles and how tough were their hearts.

They aimed as well as a banker who brings to his wife, for praise (she must), a string of golden pheasants tied by their beautiful necks. They were no less brave than a physician who calls his wife to the garage to admire (she must) a doe with long eyelashes above her beautiful eyes, opaque in death. They were as macho as two hundred pounds of redneck American in pursuit of a slender coyote. The boys were no softies, and they could take aim, as all the girls and a few sissies who stood apart could see. Then she stopped screaming.

The Third Monkey

When Derek heard, he disappeared, leaving one open suitcase behind in his bedroom. Nobody knew where to find him or if he would be back, ever. After two months he walked into the house, and Olaf told him that he could stay if he wanted to. Derek's face was drawn, but he could still contort it into a smile.

"Thank you," he said. "I'd like to. I brought some goat meat. I can bake it if you'd like." He peeled off the newspaper from the pale shank and took it outside under the tap. He was home.

From day one he tried, he tried his best, and Olaf appreciated it, because the effort was sincere, as was his occasional gloom. Derek had come with a few new habits: he had stopped going to church on Sundays, and would accept a few shots of home-made distillate, courtesy of one of the innumerable cousins of Timothy. They had a few evenings together, those evenings that make your heart sing and make life so hopeful because one is with friends. They talked politics, movies, poaching in the parks, the corruption of dictator Moi, their plans. They never discussed the past—only once, after a bottle of some suspicious toddy from the market. Derek never mentioned Lika by name. "You always lose what you love. I do. Always."

Short rains came. It cooled down, and then the first long rain arrived on March 25th. It was as miraculous as only those who wait for rains can know. The baked ground soaked up the life-bearing water in gulps and in exchange exuded that special odor that cannot be smelled any other time but when long rains come. Red eyes turned white again, the cracks in heels healed, and when one would squeeze nostrils between a thumb and forefinger and let go, the nostrils would unstick instantly. Thompson gazelles, lacquered shiny by the rain, stood by the road motionless—only their ears moved. Reebok, those deliberate antelopes, could be seen prancing by the lake, jumping up with all fours in the air, for reasons everybody understood. Girls, laughing loudly, paraded in the rain in front of Thika truckstop as if in a wet T-shirt contest, and the tough truckers watching them became suddenly quiet, with a strange expression on their faces.

Olaf conspired complicated schemes to bring home, overnight, the newly arrived schoolteacher—she was an elegant immigrant from Ethiopia. (He did not want Derek to know.) Derek traveled less, and spent hours watching the grass grow under the rain, from his window. Timothy acquired a second mistress and, long rains or not, she proved to be a complicator of his life, so he stopped by for a consult, often.

On "fool's day" in April, Olaf took his students to the playground. It was a cool morning. A soot-black cloud divided the sky in half, with its sharp purple edge preceded by a steady wind. The five knuckles of the Ngong Hills disappeared, but in the South the air was purified to such a clarity that even Kilimanjaro could be spied from a hill near Thika. Olaf was trying to gather the kids and get them inside before the downpour when he saw Timothy leaving their house. That was strange, he thought, since Timothy knew Olaf was in school that morning and that Derek would still be asleep at this hour. Timothy waved at him and walked briskly across the playground, not answering the greetings of the students. All along his way the wide smile did not leave his face.

"*Habari gani*, Olaf!"

"What's going on?" Olaf answered the greeting. "Did you win a lottery, or what?"

"Olaf, sit down, because I have a big, big surprise for you. Actually it is for Derek." Olaf did not believe in premonitions, but this time there was something that prevented him from answering Timothy's grin with a smile. "Monkey! Got a monkey!" Timothy exclaimed. "I got her from my cousin here in town. And free, man." He looked at Olaf's unsmiling face and saw it changing.

"Olaf, buddy, what is it? Can you imagine Derek? Finding her in the living room? He was still sleeping, I think, when I brought her in."

"You left the animal in there?" Olaf managed to recapture his powers of speech. "Is she in there?" He pointed at the house. Then, without waiting for an answer, he started running across the field. After a few paces he stopped, covering his mouth with his hand. An explosion had reverberated from the house: the roar of a shotgun.

The door of the house opened, and Derek appeared, barefoot and without a shirt. He did not look around, stumbling away. He walked in a straight line to the fields nearby and soon disappeared between the tall stalks of cassava, lush from the long rains.

Hearts
(A Poem)

When he left town for college, he wrote her letters about his love. On the last page he pasted pictures of hearts cut out from journals of biology, with veins and arteries, valves and ventricles in glossy colors. The poems at the end came from his heart. She wrote him back about her love in many metaphors.

When he got burnt in a trench by the sun of Da Nang, Vietnam, he glued a piece of his peeled-off skin, cut in the shape of a heart, on a homemade Valentine card. It was a good heart, and he wrote in a circle around it. She carried the Valentine with the skin-heart in her purse. She did not write back.

When he got his first job with an insurance company on the East Coast, he faxed her his longing. He drew a big heart with India ink so it would come out well on the facsimile. She was envied by the FAX operator, and she wished the operator would tell everybody.

When she married, he sent her a secret heart drawn with his urine on a white paper, without words. She remembered their games and heated the plain paper above a match—the heart appeared. She wanted to remember him, but now she could remember only his hearts.

When he married, he had a heart printed on the bottom of the wedding announcement. It was a beautiful muscle, in fresh, flaming red. She wrote him a long story, then, which she never mailed.

When he was spending his last days on the cancer ward, all the nurses wondered why he insisted on designing his own obituary.

Revenge of
Underwater Man

We had arranged to meet at the center of the Mala Strana district, at that well-worn corner where Karmelitska Street meets the square. My friends did not trust my sense of orientation yet, and they knew that one can get easily lost in the old quarters of Prague. I had been told that a few visitors get lost there every year, forever, and after only a fortnight in this city I already felt the danger of wanting to get lost, too, not to come back out to a world less magical. I felt the temptation most urgently on early mornings when the chestnut tree on the bank of the Vltava River (*Moldau fluvius*) was only a suggestion through a veil of mist, and underneath it the swans extended their wings like a schoolboy stretching in the morning, holding onto his dream of skipping school and getting lost.

I felt the urge to become forgotten here as I watched the silhouette of Hradcany Castle etched high on the hill across the river, all lit up against the blackness of the night, unreal as if copied from an old etching. I had a view of the castle, now an office of employment for the legendary Havel, from my rented apartment, so that even behind closed doors I was harassed by romantic feelings when the castle was framed by a black storm, or by curtains of rain, or was bathed in sunshine so optimistic as only a tourist pamphlet can convey. Yesterday I saw it smudged in the gun-metal gloom of an overcast sky—just to remind me, perhaps, of the gray history of this town. And to force me down from my cloud, if only briefly. However, the subsequent sunset melted my schmaltzy, soft-boiled soul and put a smile on my face which remained there for hours.

I looked forward to meeting my friends, Peter and Ivan. Petr (he spells it Peter in the U.S.) is an immigrant to Minnesota, emigrant from Prague, which he is visiting now. He has spent half his life here and half there. Ivan is a native of Prague who has remained a Prager and will be buried in the city.

"Ahoy!"

"Ahoy!"

"Ahoy!" We greeted each other. Ahoy is "Hi" for Czechs (for people who never sailed a ship and don't own even a rowboat).

"Will we eat in *Velkoprerovsky Mlyn?*" Ivan asked. "Okay then," he answered his own question. "The restaurant opens at seven, so we have some time to waste."

"Let's walk around the Kampa Park," Peter suggested. I contributed "Okay," and we wandered past the Dutch Embassy (known more for classical concerts than politics), then past the French Embassy (known less for politics than for standing across from the John Lennon Peace Wall with its graffiti portrait of Lennon). We crossed Certovka Creek, known for kayak races in recent times and for a history dating from far before the exploits of Christopher Columbus (since even creeks have a written history here). It was still light.

"Prague would wear my legs through to under my knees," Peter whined, using a literary translation of a Czech idiom. "Let's sit down somewhere!"

We found a bench with a good view of passing lovers and behind them the river and behind the river the quay with the shining Bedrich Smetana House and behind it the props of baroque domes and Gothic spires and steeples and behind them more of the ancient architecture making a skyline. The evening light supplied shades of gold to the Old Town, removing all reality. I knew this city was built of stones, not of gold.

"Wow!" I said.

An old lady passed by us, pulled by a boxer who smiled at us, then a couple of young people who stumbled because their emotions directed them to look into each other's eyes. They would barter all the town's baroque treasures for one night in an apartment of their own. That is what Ivan said, knowingly, and stretched his legs.

"What is this building over there, upstream?" I entered the conversation. "Looks in a sorry shape."

"But what a location!" Peter remarked.

"That's Sovuv Mill, an old mill. And you are right about the location. Big bucks, enormous investments in steak." Ivan suggested support of a large object with his hands. "Can you imagine making that into a first-class hotel? Right on the river and with those views?"

"Is that why it's in such rotten shape? Because it is in such a great place?" Peter smiled.

"Exactly! Government, foreign companies, pre-communist owners—they are all boxing each other for it. So while everything historical around here is getting fixed and spruced up, the mill is rotting—because it is ancient and sits on such a knock-out location." Ivan nodded contently, liking the absurdity, as all his compatriots do.

And looking for more of the absurd, he added, after a while: "and those two lovers, over there?" He pointed at the couple walking away. "The fellow will not make love skillfully to her tonight." I must have looked puzzled, since Ivan turned to me with an explanation. "You saw his face, didn't you? Too much in love with her."

Now Peter joined in with a short lecture: "And also, because the grass is wet tonight." I resisted revealing my puzzlement. Still, Peter explained with mock patience, the lovers will walk 'round and 'round the park waiting for the descent of darkness, since darkness will be their roof, and the lawn their bed, and the bushes their walls, and the blossoms on the bushes pictures on the walls.

"They wouldn't be able to switch off the moon, so they hope for a cloudy night, romance or not. Police, you know," Ivan added, looking at the sky. He laughed at my lack of understanding of the world of Prague around me. Even Peter knew everything, despite having lived on another planet, Minnesota, for a quarter of a century. Both my friends lit cigarettes and exchanged a few sentences in that horrible language of theirs.

"Sorry." Ivan looked at me and switched to his accented but quite precise English. "Sovuv Mill? Did you ask about its history? I don't know much about it, but I am certain about one thing—there used to be a Vodnik living right under the mill; that has been passed on since the old times."

"V o d n i k ?" I tried the pronunciation.

"Right, Vodnik," Peter agreed with Ivan. "Ivan, tell him. They call it the 'Land of Ten Thousand Lakes,' where he and I are living in the States. He should know."

And that is how I came to know about the underwater man.

Vodnik

"Mythical fellow, fairytale character, that Vodnik." Ivan started without hesitation. "Sometimes he has been called Hastrman. A great diver. Underwaterman, you could say."

Revenge of Underwater Man   45

Ivan seemed to have graduated with distinction from grandmother's school of fairy tales. In detail, he knew the dress code of this Vodnik: always in a green tailcoat, a red cap and, on special occasions, a green top hat, with red boots. He has punk-green, long hair, webbed toes, and fingers like a newt. He favors whiskers, catfish-style. On the rare instances when he has talked to people, he seemed to have a speech defect, a nasality combined with lisping.

He inhabits an underwater shelter, of course, usually in the deep under a mill or in the deepest part of a lake or forest pond. He savors his leisure time. At night, when the moon is full, he climbs up a willow tree growing on the bank, lights his pipe, and mends his boots. Water drips from the left tail of his coat. It is always the left tail. So many people have seen him in this position on the willow that there remain no doubts about his appearance. Those who have seen him have been mostly peasants returning home from the tavern of a neighboring village at night, which might raise questions about the reliability of their perceptions—but they have all sworn it was true, nothing but the truth, their own living eyes saw him there.

The lovers passed by on their rounds around the park again, and the man still radiated a confusion of love from his eyes. Somewhere on their circle he had managed to unbutton the upper part of her blouse.

"Do you want to hear more about Czech mythology or not?" Ivan saw my interest in the progress of the lovers.

"Oh yeah, Ivan. Be my grandma, please!" I asked him then, if he, Vodnik, could be considered a good guy, a moral, positive example to youth.

"Well, *entre nous,* Vodnik drowns people, you know?" Ivan continued in a portentous voice, with relish. "Sometimes. He pulls them underwater, tangles them into the shoots of a pond lily, and doesn't release the body for three days. Three! And—this is important—he keeps their souls. Forever. I think the human soul looks like the air bladder of a carp, about the same size, too. He puts that soul into a clay jar which he covers with a heavy lid. All Vodniks are very proud of their collection of souls."

"So, he is a pretty lily-livered evil spirit, isn't he?"

"There is a problem here." Ivan put on a victorious expression. Absurdity again? "We just cannot say that. You see, he helps people, sometimes. I don't know his chromosomes, but he ain't no congenital meanie. For a couple of beers he would help the working folks in the mill; he might do the jobs of twenty, overnight. It is when he gets mad, when he sees there is no percentage in being good, then it is just drowning, nothing but drowning. He would hang colored ribbons on the bushes along the pond and kids would try to get at them and—whoops—another soul on the shelves in the jar collection."

"How about his sex life?" Peter asked, as I would have expected, knowing him for many years. "He seems to have the lifestyle of a couple of my bachelor friends. Except that drowning part, I think."

Ivan changed his diction to a professorial tone: "Sometimes, he kidnaps a shapely maiden—keeps her for years. Understandable. But he also has a wife, Hastrmanka!"

"And Hastrmanka, the wife?"

"She has three main characteristics. One, she is ugly. Two, she can't cook. Three, she is sneaky. Sound familiar?" he laughed, which, I thought, might have revealed something about his life experiences.

"Often, she changes into a frog or a toad and sneaks close to women working in the fields to listen to what they say. She must be a lonely creature." Ivan looked at his watch. "They are opening the restaurant. How about going?"

Walking toward Velkoprerovsky Mlyn, we met the lovers again. There had been no progress with her blouse buttons, so I turned my mind back to contemplating Vodnik, another of those Czech personalities whose behavior intrigued me with its ambiguity. I became determined to understand better why in Bohemian ponds and forests a peasant could not bear a fairytale character who would be straightforwardly evil, like a cannibalistic grandmother, or one positively lovely and politically correct, like Snow White. Would I be able to find out, to understand these titillating Bohunks?

The Restaurant

The restaurant set right on the bank of Certovka Creek and from the window, next to our table, we could observe the enormous wheel of Velkoprerovsky Mill, after which the restaurant was named. The wheel had been nicely restored for the tourists' sake; it even moved and creaked, driven by the India-ink stream. I ordered fried breaded carp and cucumber salad with sweetened vinegar. In having the carp I wanted to impress my friends and, indeed, they expressed surprise at my audacity. The second reward for me was its taste, which was delicate, non-fishy, and pleasantly adventurous.

The wine was a Moravian Muller-Thurgau white from Hodonin. It was a thin, slightly acidic, unremarkable fluid, but revered by natives (with raised eyebrows, puckered lips, and smacking sounds).

Peter explained this lack of objectivity, with a dose of sarcasm, as due to the defeat of Czech nobles on Bila Hora in 1620—and the resulting three centuries of darkness, which had deprived the nation of the opportunity to learn of the Grand Crus wines of Bordeaux and the great white vintages of the Mosel region. Indeed, our first glass of wine was a mediocre experience, but it got clearly better with each subsequent glass and bottle we downed. I commented on this phenomenon with surprise, only to be informed that it had been observed by King Charles IV and a fellow by the name of Busek from Vilhartice in the fourteenth century already.

"... And, also, its taste depends greatly on the drinker's company and their feelings of friendship toward each other. This, of course, defies the international criteria used in judging wines. Pity," said Ivan. We had achieved the spirit of special camaraderie after the third bottle, I think, drinking to Vodnik, just the same. But the restaurant was closing, and the waiters were leaning the chairs so that their backs would rest on the edges of the tables. I understood that this position for chairs signified a physical exclamation mark at the end of hours.

"Hauuuw How How, don't do it!" Ivan howled dismay that we had to leave; then he calmed down. "You have two options now." He turned to me. "The first option is to go home and have that healthy sleep. The second: to dive into a smoke-filled tavern to try another vintage of Moravian—and to hear me telling my personal story about Vodnik. A true one." Then he looked at Peter as if giving him permission to decide for me.

Peter did not hesitate: "Be it Vodnik! No question about that." Peter looked at my face for traces of rebellion.

"Sure thing," I said loudly, feeling native and proud of it. "Sure thing." Czechs don't separate when a story is imminent, regardless of the hour. I read that.

The Tavern

It seemed we actually dove in—the stairs were so steep into the underground hall, filled with blue smoke, as promised by Ivan. Storytellers saturated the space with vehement voices; wine flowed in the hive. We found a place at a table of darkened oak planks so heavy no drunk had ever even tilted it. It was pleasant to lean on it. My friends commented on the rieslingoid acidity of the green Veltlin Moravian we ordered, and exchanged greetings, or insults(?), with strangers at the next table.

"I am warning you. There isn't much tender romance at the end of THIS Vodnik story." Then Ivan told us about his tender romance with Lida Zabranska.

"She was the second most beautiful girl in our school. She was put together a little awkwardly, perhaps: everything was long about her. Her arms were a bit too slender, her legs like a gazelle's, even her face was Anglo-Saxon, and her breasts were long, too, with narrow bases—not a bright future for them, but in the good old times of tight sweaters it was something to get dizzy about." Ivan remedied the sudden dryness of his tongue with a gulp of green Veltlin.

"She was different. Never wore any makeup, not even lipstick and, I think, this was one of the reasons I can still remember her eyes, which radiated in that unpainted, alabaster face. Pure milk chocolate with pupils as wide as if atropine had done it. I can tell you I used to get lost in those eyes. Just lost, no way out.

"I was seventeen, and she was one grade lower. At that age a woman can look like an angel still. But there were these rumors circulating in the hallways of the school that she was not one of the angels, which only enhanced my shyness, and it took me a year before I joined her on the way home from school. Then she let me pay for the movie. It was *Rhapsody in Blue*, and there I held her hand. Vole!

"On Sunday afternoons we went to the 'Tea,' to the tea dance in the gym up in Hanspaulka. She would wear a pink dress of imitation silk, tight around her waist and high to the lace collar around that Modigliani neck. You wouldn't believe it, but I remember clearly, still today, how her waist felt against my sweaty palm, and when we slow-danced to "Moonlight Serenade," how I bent myself forward so my hips wouldn't touch hers, and how she pulled me closer, and I felt her breasts, which made me all burning and confused, and then, how my schoolwork went straight to hell, and I almost flunked that year.

"I am not sure, now, if I was in love because she was so beautiful, or if she appeared so beautiful because I was in love. It bothers me now, but comes as no surprise, that I cannot resurrect that feeling, but I know it was an emotion of such power and purity that the gods allow it only in a single dose and only to a selected few innocents. It even prevented me from kissing her, which is always an irreparable mistake.

"And then, one day, she disappeared from school. Gone. Just like that. It took me lots of detective work to find out that her parents had put her in an all-female monastic boarding school of the Vorsilki Order. A fucking prison, if you ask me. Sorry," Ivan said, pouring himself some more.

The waiter brought another bottle and leaned over the table to hear more about a prison. Peter waved him away. I noticed that the Veltlin green was getting better, as expected, and that it had put a permanent smile on Peter's face. The still handsome, somewhat dark features of Ivan showed only the concentration required to revive the memories. He pushed his Minnesota Twins cap (a present from Peter) backwards.

"She was gone and unreachable, which must have been a blow to me. But, frankly, I don't remember it well. One of those mechanisms which the brain uses to suppress bad events from the memory, to keep us dreaming without nightmares, must have been triggered later. Anyway, about a year passed, and I still had this longing, like a pain here, in the heart, still not diminished, not even a little.

"Then one Sunday evening I found myself collecting fossils, alone and lonely, on the Barrandov Silurian cliffs on the outskirts of Prague (our Secret Paleontology Club had disintegrated). Despite finding an undamaged specimen of a trilobite and an orthoceras, I wandered back to the tram station without joy, thinking about Lida locked in the Vorsilky Monastery. I decided to take a detour by tram to see the place, the Monastery. Should I scream her name at the windows? Or should I ring at the gate and tell the nun gatekeeper that I carried a message of great importance for Lida Zabranska. Or some other bullshit. Or simply beg to see her? Maybe?

"I got off the tram in front of the National Theatre and walked half a block to Vorsilky School. It was dark already, but the door of the Monastery's cathedral was open. I could see the lights inside; it was filled with people. So I crawled in, found a place near the aisle, wondering what might be happening at this late hour. I hoped she might be around somewhere; I would have even prayed for that, if I had known how.

"The organ music filling the space suddenly acquired more celebratory decibels. There was a commotion in the pews, and people turned their heads toward the side entrance; some half-raised from their seats. By twos, a procession of young women in white, floor-length robes was entering, slowly; their eyes turned down to the marble floor. In their right hands they held candles with flickering flames. They were like angels on hidden wheels, since one could not perceive their steps. Only an occasional glance to the side by some made them humanly alive. No smiles were offered.

"Then Lida appeared. She was taller than the others and attracted stares from the audience. She passed by me three, four feet away, and did not see me. She had managed to put on the face of an angel, a face so beautiful it stays with me till today, veiled only slightly. She put on a small, brittle smile, a suggestion of a smile enhancing that amazing beauty.

"Her eyes were turned down, but just before she approached me she looked up, and I could see clearly how those eyes were narrowed, telling all who watched her that she hated this show, that she didn't belong here. That is how I interpreted it. There was a little mist in those eyes, and that pained me then. I whispered something, but she did not hear me. She had no notion I was right by her. And that was the last time I saw her, gentlemen, the last time for years.

"Later I learned that she was dismissed from the Monastery School, that she tried to escape over the border to Germany with her parents. They were caught; her parents were put in prison, and she had to work at a forced labor assignment in a clothing factory in Northern Bohemia. I lost track of her fate."

The Stairs

"What a deal!" Peter said.

"Thank you, Ivan," I mumbled, moved a little, I admit. We sat in silence for a while. The acidity of the green wine had disappeared from its taste completely, by then. I tried to order open-faced sandwiches for everybody, in Czech, but the waiter gave me a blank stare.

"But Vodnik? Where has he been?" asked Peter, a little tipsy, spilling some of his wine, since while Ivan had been talking we had drunk his share.

"Well, don't worry about him," said Ivan. "He will come if you want to hear about him. Outside. Look around, and you'll see we are here alone." The waiters were tipping up the chairs so they would lean with their back-rests on the edge of the tables, and the place was empty. We paid (went Dutch), thanked them, and promised to come again soon.

The street was deserted. Not far from us we could see the sprawling stairs of St. Nicholas Church. I carried the unfinished bottle of liquid sun from Moravia. We spread out on the church steps, passed the bottle around, and Ivan and Peter shared their last cigarette. I took my shoes off and hyperventilated the fresh air.

"So, Ivan!" Peter motioned with his hand.

"It was about five years ago. I met her, Lida, on Charles Square," Ivan started. "I was sitting on a bench watching the bronze orchid in the bronze hand of the statue of Rossler. Something obstructed my view, and there she stood in front of me, with a smile. I recognized her right away, after all those years, and called her name.

"Ivan, Ivanku!" she said.

"I will not describe her, since you know how unkindly time works on tissues. She had aged, of course." (We gave Ivan the last of the wine. I wished I could get him a cigarette, or something good. It seemed he had difficulty in continuing, so we just waited.)

"We talked about nonsense while we found a table in an espresso place near Faust's house. We talked about high school—the usual. I could see she was not uneasy with me at all, which made me sad, a little. She had forgotten we'd had a date, once. And I did not tell her. Did not mention Vorsilky, either. So we followed the chronology of her life, the common milestones of marriage, two kids, jobs, hopes found and lost and found again.

"We ate open-faced sandwiches and drank espresso and ate 'rakvicky,' pastry coffins filled with cream. Then a strange thing happened. While we talked and time passed, I noticed that her face was changing, that she looked younger and younger and more familiar. The metamorphosis made me feel a little confused, and I decided I did not want this meeting to finish as plainly as was her story, so far. I wanted to hear the real stuff about her. If there was any. About her insides, because she was going to disappear again, maybe forever.

"I found the courage to ask her: 'Have you ever been in love, Lida? Like, really in love?' She was surprised. She did not look at me, twirled the coffee in her cup. Then she talked with her eyes on the cup, as if she were reading the past, not the future, from the coffee grounds.

"'So, I tell you, Ivan.' She whispered it. 'It was a long time ago, it seems. He wrote for me:

> trees laugh at the thunder
> air scented after hope like you
> rain covers your face with a hundred happy tears
> narrows your eyes, wets your lips to be mine.

'I still remember it. For a poet he did everything right: long hair to his shoulders, a sad jacket, and his shirt buttoned all the way; no tie. Even his cheeks he kept hollow, and he coughed, too. I thought: of course, he is my eternal love, the first and the last one.'"

A few drops of rain rang on our heads. I looked up at the immense gilded cliffs of St. Nicholas Cathedral looming above us, at the sleeping palaces across the square, and wished the story would not end soon. I looked at Ivan's face. When the end of the story comes, let it be a happy end, please, I wished. The story continued, mercilessly.

The poet had written Lida letters full of metaphors so strange she could not understand most of them. But the yearning in the poems she understood, because when he recited them for her, he held her hands and looked at her with eyes so narrow she thought his verses must be beautiful and only for her. Sometimes, he seemed to be a child, laughing at silly things, a child with tantrums and little evil jokes. But his eyes were never the eyes of a child. The time came when the eyes did not look at her when he recited his poems. And then, one evening, she saw him looking into the eyes of another young woman, holding her in his arms, leaning on the railing of the quay across Rudolphinum. She went to pieces, then somewhat pulled herself together and within a few months was married to Rudi, engineer Rudi Skala.

The truth is, she had never recovered. She used to fall into a depression every year; something had always been pulling her down. She saw those eyes of the poet; she heard his verses and could not understand why the passing of time did not help her, as it should. It did not console her that Rudi was a solid man: he was liked by his many friends; he loved their two boys, and they loved him; he took good care of all of them, and he was kind to her and worried about her.

At last, she found a doctor whom she could trust and who would listen to her with compassion. The old medicine man prescribed long vacations, without kids, in South Bohemia, preferably in a village, far from the city, from the bullshit of her work and from being hounded by crowds. Only the two of them, Rudi and her.

They rented an old farmhouse at the edge of a village, with a creek running through the garden and a private spring-well in the cellar, where a pair of blue salamanders lurked. The neighbor's sheepdog became their faithful friend and would follow them on their excursions. Daily they woke up to the sun; the meadows were warm, and dizzied them with colors. They walked through them from the village to the town market. They picked boletus mushrooms in the pine forest up the hill and made picnics by the cross in the fields, from which Jesus watched them with a smirk, suspicious but kind. Rudi was also kind, as usual, but now he laughed with her, and often he held her hand. For the first time in years, she felt unshackled, as if freed from an exile in some icy, confusing world.

On the last day of their vacation, she prepared a special dinner of mushrooms they had collected in the pine forest, and Rudi made a tomato salad fragrant with herbs from the meadow. Pleasure-bearing endorphins flooded their brains. They entrusted to the salamanders in the spring-well in the cellar two bottles of wine to cool for later, in anticipation of a romantic night. After dinner they went for a walk in a breeze which carried the perfume of the fields and touched them as softly as velvet. At the edge of the forest they observed a pair of deer, motionless as theater props, as if enchanted by the scented wind, too.

They entered the forest, and on a narrow path they walked hand in hand to the pond she loved. They sat down on the shore by the clump of reeds. There were pond lilies at one end. There was a moss-covered shallows with tiny white flowers clumped in pillows, arrow-arums blooming next to the cattails and a willow tree. A solitary willow.

She knew this pond well. In the evening one could spy a muskrat there. Sometimes, in the morning, a white heron would keep his vigil near the mossy shallows, a merciless killer of frogs disguised in a white shroud of innocence. She believed him innocent. The surface of the pond would change each time Lida visited here. She liked it most when it mirrored a summer cloud. That night, the last night of their vacation, the surface was dark with ripples, making it shiver as if alive. Rudi took her hand.

"Rudi," she whispered. "Look at the willow. Do you recognize it?"

"What do you mean?" he asked.

"This is the willow Vodnik will climb on." Her voice was barely audible; her face had a tiny smile of conspiracy. "I can almost see him. On that branch leaning over the pond. He might come out if we are really quiet."

Rudi nodded, looking at the willow. She put her arm around his waist. "When it gets a little darker he will emerge, mend his shoes—and maybe, play his flute." She whispered and cuddled with him. She felt, she knew, that he shared the happiness with her. The breeze died; the silence was complete. "It is our fairy tale, Rudi."

She looked at him. He wore a navy blue sweater with a turtle-neck. His profile was so handsome, with a strong nose and the chin of a decisive man, and dark, unruly hair falling over his forehead, with a few white streaks in it now.

"Rudi?"

He turned to her and smiled. "Let's get out of here!" he said. "It smells like shit here. Somebody did it here, somewhere. Holy shit!"

Ivan stretched his legs over the steps of St. Nicholas Cathedral. Peter and I, we looked at him, but he showed no emotion. Just turned his head from side to side as if wondering. He asked for a cigarette, but there were none left.

"It's getting late," Ivan said, after a while. "Or early. I've heard the first morning tram already. But, I have to tell you, drunks: you have listened well. Real well."

We got up. "What happened to her, Ivan?" I asked, taking care to sound casual.

"Yeah, right, you should know. After that Vodnik incident, she disintegrated, of course, totally. No sleep, no food, didn't talk. Finally, her husband, the master of sensitivity, had to commit her to the looney house.

"After a couple of months the shrinks got the better of her, and she went back to old Rudi and her two boys. There were no choices for her, simply no choices. She became a sort of regular homemaker, as you would say in America. She remained slightly zombied out, but that only helped her to exist. Then Rudi died on her, of a heart attack. The old sport." We were walking to the other side of St. Nicholas to the tram station.

"She got over his death pretty well; the empty space he left behind was quite small. That's how life goes, right?" He imitated a brief laugh. "And that is the 'revenge of Vodnik' for you."

"Have you seen her since she told you this?" I asked. Ivan's face widened in a big smile, a wide smile with no eyes. The first one in the last hour.

"Oh yeah. I have seen her, since," he said, his grin still on, only with the eyes, now. "Peter, here, he saw her too. And likes her cooking. Don't ya, Peter?"

Peter laughed. They both looked at me victoriously, and I was standing there like an idiot, not comprehending what was going on.

"But don't worry, you'll meet her, ma gal, my wife! Tomorrow for dinner, as we have arranged," said Ivan. "I bet you'll agree that Lida is the master of knedliky, roast pork and sauerkraut." Ivan was still grinning. "And fun, too."

The Bridge

We came to the Malostranske Square tram station. Both Peter and Ivan insisted I should take a shortcut over the bridge and not wait with them for the tram. You need to get to bed fast, they said, to dream a Czech dream about Vodnik in living color; and they pointed my way toward Charles Bridge.

I went down Mostecka Street, past the McDonalds set in a house three hundred years old near the Bridge Tower, six hundred years old. It was getting lighter. The pre-dawn light allowed me to read the clock in the tower. The clock told me it was true that friends in this city can sit down and talk for ten hours without interruption, and then feel sorry they have to part. I did.

From under the Tower I emerged, suddenly, on the Charles Bridge. The magic of the view glued my soles to the cobblestones. The bridge, veiled in fog rising from the river, seemed to lead to dreams. The statues of saints emerging from the fog walked slowly toward me. When I stepped forward to meet them, they stopped and looked away.

There was nobody on the bridge except me and the seagulls. They were landing on the statues of the saints, knitting snow-white caps for the stony heads with their excrement. The whitest seemed to be the one decorating the forehead of Saint Jan Nepomuk, who was crudely drowned here, centuries ago. And whose soul, saint or no saint, rests in one of the clay jars with a heavy lid in Vodnik's shelter, in the deep, under the bridge. I stopped near Saint Nepomuk and leaned over the side, stealthily, not to make any fast moves. I scanned the surface of the river like a spy. There was a sudden movement on the icebreaker, then a splash ... and suspicious circles spread on the surface of the ancient stream.

Billy's Last Smoke

Billy decided to have a last smoke. It did not matter, anyway; he was sure by now that it would be the last one here, that he would start packing tonight. Life had not been too bad at the U. He had been employed by The Midwestern University for a short enough time to feel a sense of belonging, but long enough to make for himself a reputation as a nice guy, a near-fatal repute in any University, an established fact that Billy did not comprehend. He was lucky in not understanding well the ways of politics, and being lucky he had been happy in fulfilling the three Commandments of Academia: teaching, research, and service. Sadly, his contentment had ended, effective the first of December. That date had done him in permanently, because that was when The Midwestern University started to enforce the correctly intentioned, multiculturally all-encompassing, bizarre regulation banning smoking even in front of the buildings and on the Mall.

On December 7th, the week after the fateful date of the first of December, he had untied his woolen tie, stretched it and, with care, tucked it into the thin space under his office door. Not even a trace of smoke, not even a treacherous whiff, would escape into the corridor. Windows closed: check; door locked: check. Billy disliked this gray formica door. He had to watch it constantly to be sure it stayed open. It was in the regulations that all staff had to memorize, that "80 percent of time spent in the office must be devoted to work on grant applications. This ruling will be enforced and monitored by University Surveillance Troops (UST), using spot-checks. To facilitate the duties of our USTs, the office door must be open at least 45 degrees at all times."

Billy's door was locked, now, in defiance of the standing order, and he allowed his mind to wander. He could visualize the door of Dad's house in Montana. Made of Douglas fir, it smelled of resin, smoke, and time; when moved, it sang, not squeaked, in three tones, clear like the tune of a violin bird. The image of a zinc patch over the bullet hole above the doorknob made him homesick now. That home seemed far, far away, in miles and in time, too. Outside, heavy, wet snowflakes tumbled down, announcing the imminent shopping frenzy of Christmas and, at his distant home, the great 2001 New Year's Eve party. There was something to look forward to in a couple of weeks, but not in thirty minutes. Only half an hour was left before the hearing.

The water was boiling for coffee. He added almost two spoonfuls of fine grounds to his cup, and a spoonful of brown sugar, pulled out the lowest drawer of the desk, and from under the pile of reprints of his publications he recovered a pack of Dunhill cigarettes. He put one cigarette under his nose and smelled the tobacco, a sun-filled, warm scent, unlike the fragrance of any blossom he knew. He laid the cigarette under his nose horizontally, lifted his upper lip, and let go. The curled lip held the cigarette under his nose. He smiled—and then it fell off into his hand.

Billy took a sip of coffee "to dissolve the mucus," as he used to say, before lighting the cigarette. He leaned back in his chair, letting the smoke escape, first, through his nose and then, pouting his lips, he blew the rest in a clean milky stream without turbulence. In the still air of the room the smoke rose to the ceiling, where it dissolved in changing patterns: whirls and winding streams with their own life, independent of the smoker.

After the last smoke Billy extinguished the butt and hid the crystal ashtray, still with ashes, in the space under the heating duct. He knew it would have been a mistake to dump the ashes into the wastebasket, remembering the important function of UST in checking the garbage for information. Now, again, Billy started to feel fear as a heaviness in his belly and a slight pain in the middle of his chest. He was well aware that his hopes for L.T.—limited tenure—were surely gone and his days of employment were numbered in single digits.

To achieve L.T. had been his greatest aspiration for five years at the University. It meant a quite permanent position (subject to yearly review by UST and the Executive Committee, of the applicant's sexual activity—limited to one legal partner, his avoidance of alcohol and tobacco, his Effort Certification, and his regular attendance at Self-Criticism Drills, Multicultural Sensitivity Training Workshops, and Desexualization Retreats). Appointment would be terminated instantly, of course, in any case in which the use of controlled substances had been suspected. The most recent instance of such termination was the infamous Tolarski case. One fateful evening, that physicist had been observed engaged in a mating ritual on a laboratory table with an employee of the opposite gender, his girlfriend, while consuming half a bottle of Swiss Colony red wine (a foreign import, according to UST) and smoking almost a pack of cigarettes.

Actually, Billy knew this fellow Tolarski. He was a funny guy, always humming a tune, grinning happily about something, so Billy had already suspected that he might come to a rotten end. And he did. He could have been just expelled from the School, but his girlfriend, a year after his termination, had revealed that she had not given him written permission for his act of love. Now he was putting into practice his erudition in physics as a segment of the chain gang at Calmwater Prison. Billy shuddered at the thought.

———

All the members of the Commission were in the conference room already when Billy hunched in. All except Chairperson Bolbolian. He was lingering in his office watching the clock, in order to arrive exactly ten minutes late.

Curak was sitting opposite Billy in a brown jacket, polyester slacks, brown shoes. His narrow lips, thin nose, and beady eyes formed the motionless, somewhat sclerotic mask of a "reasonable man." Curak was good, just, and reasonable, and notorious for derailing the academic future of many a student and incipient colleague, with his correct judgment and goodness. He had been striving for the victory of high moral principles for thirty years, and since the morality of humans is known to be suspect, he was disliked by almost every suspect. Curak nodded at Billy. Like a praying mantis, Billy thought. "Good day my friend," said Curak. "Good day to you."

Schonheit sat next to him, leaning back, his permanent smile on. He beamed in his new, wildly checkered jacket, a conversation piece he called Esterhazy with an all-knowing grin ("imported directly from Budapest, Poland!"). Schonheit was a soft kind of a porky fella. His skin was soft; the remnants of his hair, his voice, his handshake were really soft. But Billy knew he was like the soft-shelled turtle, that cousin of an alligator snapper, with a soft shell but dangerous jaws. Schonheit had made it in the administration in the same carnivorous way that the soft-shelled *Trionyx ferox* makes it, in the strange kingdom of a swamp. "Shall we take a straw vote?" he said, but nobody paid attention. He nodded with his head slightly askew, acknowledging Billy.

The third member of the Commission, Olson, pulled out a notebook and placed a sharp pencil precisely parallel to it, avoiding the eyes of Billy and everybody else. And nobody looked at him, since he did not have a face. This had always struck Billy as strange: no eyes, no mouth and nose, no face. His language was complex, incomprehensible and verbose and full of words with Latin roots and ambiguous meanings, so he functioned very well and was much in demand as a member of many important committees, where he never once failed to vote with the majority, and never expressed his opinion in a way that could be interpreted one way and not the other. Thus, in effect, his presence diminished the number on any committee by one, and at the same time increased the vote for the majority by one. There were numerous faceless administrators at the U, but Olson was the one quoted most often in the correctly amateurish *Midwestern Daily*.

Now Bolbolian jogged into the room, words jetting from his mouth in an even stream. He was the Chairperson (with only a vaguely recognizable sexual identity to be called Chairman or Chairwoman). Also, it had been rumored that he was gutless and spineless, but both of these attributes, Billy knew, should have been anatomically impossible. Yes, there were members of the faculty who believed that Bolbolian did not have a spine, but while it had been possible in such individuals to maintain posture by using implanted titanium rods, in Bolbolian's case spinelessness had not been proven beyond any unreasonable doubt. It was common knowledge that he had been nominated to chair the Commission for his unfailing eagerness to represent those judicious men of high morals who wielded the real power in the School. Now he spoke, modulating his voice with the deliberation and gravity of a philosopher.

"It is so wonderful to meet with you today, my friends. By the way, I have been thinking this morning that I will propose a new motto for the School. Really, believe me comrades, I am quite excited about it—because of its depth and originality. I dare say. Listen to this: 'Do not ask the School what she can do to you. Ask yourself, instead, what you can do for the School!'

"Now, isn't that something? This thought came to me while praying." He hung his head with unfelt humility. "Oh my! But let us begin, so that we will not inconvenience our dear friend Billy here, and we can all go back to hard work, to contributing to the reputation of our alma mater, to attracting more funds for research and for our administration. And teaching." His toupee moved slightly.

Curak decided to bring up the agenda at this moment. "Comrades, I'd like to bring up the agenda at this moment." Billy got that sinking feeling, again. "Before we come to the serious charges against Comrade Billy, I must read to you, verbatim, the ruling by our Provost for Health and Morals: 'smoking of tobacco and other poisonous substances is not permitted near building entrances. Ashtrays at entrances are intended for visitors to use to extinguish cigarettes immediately, prior to entering the building.' Immediately, comrades; extinguish immediately. And urns are already in place!"

Billy? Billy almost choked. Urns! An image of an urn with his ashen remains flashed on a screen in his brain.

"Smoking urns, that is," added Curak, without moving his thin lips. "This ruling was activated on December 1, and our USTs, with the collaboration of volunteer cadres and people, has been authorized by the authorities to observe, follow, and denounce violators." He took a sip of Diet Rite. "So here we have the boilerplate. Boiler."

The flat front of Olson's skull, where ordinarily a face is formed in humans, slowly rotated toward Billy. Schonheit's face also turned. A soft smile. The room was free of sound. "Boilerplate," Curak broke in again.

Chairperson Bolbolian realized that in half an hour he had an appointment to interview, for the second time, an applicant for a secretarial position. He liked her positive attitude and physical attributes. He had to speed up the meeting. "Let us come to the charges, so that we can fairly and squarely proceed, early in the process of instigating and perpetuating the fascist.... I'm sorry, the fascinating and humane rules and regulating of ... anyway." He looked in the direction of Olson, thinking *I bet that butt-faced loser did forget the papers with the charges sent from UST headquarters.* "Anyway, Olson, Comrade, could you kindly recite the charges without delay, in due process?"

From that faceless skull a hollow voice with a deep timbre resonated in the air of the conference room, equally in all directions: "On December 4th, in the year 2001, the member of the junior faculty known as William, alias Billy, during the twenty-minute period allotted for the consumption of the midday meal, approached the building called Deer Hall from the North and leaned on the maidenhair tree approximately twenty yards from the actual wall of the building. He lighted a cigarette and publicly exhaled the smoke into the atmosphere. Observers from UST at the scene, and four volunteer witnesses, hereby attest to this act of flagrant, fragrant violation. The discarded remnant of the cigarette (the butt) was retrieved. Please find it in the enclosed plastic container, as an article of evidence."

Sweat appeared on Billy's forehead, like tiny transparent pearls which grew in size, then descended in winding streams to hide in his eyebrows. Billy couldn't hide. Then it happened. Billy's hand released its spastic grip on his knee, rose up, and the hand pulled out a cigarette from the shirt pocket. Involuntarily, his other hand lit the cigarette—and Billy inhaled, and followed it with an exhalation. Three pairs of enlarged eyes watched the smoke in fascination.

Billy reacted first to that incredible betrayal by his hands with an action which, later, would be described as a panic reaction in the records of the termination process. He spit the cigarette into the wastebasket, in which a few discarded papers ignited instantly. Bolbolian tore the fire extinguisher off the wall, activated it, and pointed it with a dramatic gesture at the fire. Nothing happened. Schonheit, seeing his chance, removed his Esterhazy jacket and, with a patriotic howl, threw it over the wastebasket to cover the flames. They died.

Peace descended on all, as when a campfire has died and only cinders remain to glow in the dark. Thus peace overcame Billy—nostalgic and almost sleepy relief. All the commissioners had disappeared without a word, by now. The magnitude of Billy's transgression did not merit their comment.

The door filled with the bulk of Schonheit. A wide smile radiated on his soft face. He whispered softly, "Gotcha, fucka!" and disappeared. Billy was alone, again. There was no percentage in being a good boy, now, so he lighted another cigarette with a smoldering piece of paper from the wastebasket. His life would change. And all he had ever wished for was a bearable lightness of being. That was all he desired.

Holding high his Dunhill calumet of peace, he blew smoke first to the East, then to the North, and to the South. He inhaled another drag and blew a straight stream of dreamy-blue smoke Westward, over the Mississippi River, past the muddy Missouri, over the snowy camelbacks of the Rockies, Westward to home. *What the hell,* he thought, *the New Year's Eve party is coming soon, anyway. It will be in J.J.'s place, the rowdiest in Helena, and everybody will be there, I reckon. Everybody. And Billy, free me.*

Yoroshiku

I tried to remember all the meanings of the word. The first time I heard "yoroshiku onegaishimasu" was in a village bar in Kamikawa, high in the mountains of the great Kawabata's "Snow Country." It is a day's drive from Niigata, around Sanjo-shi and then up into the hills on a winding road through forests that become wilder with increasing elevation and make you doubt that Japan is supposed to suffer from overpopulation.

I thought about the meaning of *yoroshiku*, but it was hard to concentrate, sitting by the window in *shinkansen*, the bullet train from Niigata through Tokyo to Kyoto. The most photogenic countryside I have known rushed by, a hundred miles an hour, and the scenes changed with the pace of a movie run at twice the proper speed. We passed small hamlets, their architecture unchanged for centuries; passed houses of sun-aged timber with roofs of aquamarine tiles glazed shiny as if after a rain; then ran along growths of shamrock-green bamboo and small cedar forests losing the battle with rice-paddies of impeccable geometry, crisscrossed by narrow asphalt roads. The occasional stream, always stony and of untamed course, whispered messages about a wilderness up in the mountains on the horizon.

Yoroshiku: it means "take care of me well in the future, please," "be kind and generous to me," "open your heart to friendship between us." Mostly it means friendship—but there is more to it. I hoped it would come to me later. I ordered green tea with rice cookies from a cute vendor in a strict uniform, reclined the back of my posh seat, and leaned back. What an evening yesterday, what a night!

I could not remember how many bottles of sake we had finished or how many hours it had taken. The big woman who runs the bar in Kamikawa village could barely keep up the pace, warming the little carafes with a bamboo pattern on them painted in the *sumi-e* style. She served us bums, smiling and on her knees to the very end, that gracious lady. Yunichi had got red in the face right away, I remember that, but the other fellow who joined us, his first name was Akira, he had kept a steady hold on his sake cups throughout the night.

Yunichi has been my old and true friend for many years, I am proud to say. He is a great poet, a traveled and educated man of sensitive heart. Akira is an official in the village government of Kamikawa, so with multiple bows and sucking in of air he had showed a heap of respect, at first, but soon loosened his tie and shyness, and from his beefy forehead the wrinkles disappeared. He admired, expertly, the craftsmanship in the pottery of the carafes. "Poetry," he had mispronounced.

It might have been this slip of the tongue that had reminded Yunichi of his passion, and he had knelt and recited his poem (I had copied it down carefully) about a woman he'd met on the train coming here to Kamikawa:

> Page from a magazine
> Michiko folded
> over and over
> till an origami crane
> lay in my hand.
>
> Then, with a bow,
> a petal of chrysanthemum
> vanished forever
> in Nagaoka station.
>
> The paper crane,
> sad wings,
> still on my palm.

He pronounced each word slowly, on his knees, his arms motionless by his upright trunk, like a soldier kneeling at attention. A tear ran down his face, which was very beautiful.

We poured sake into those tiny cups for each other, according to the customs of politeness, and spilled only a little. We downed them, chanting "kampai," at first, but after a couple of hours we drank only to "yoroshiku." And the "gaijin," the foreign Occidental, that's me, had started to feel his heart opening. I had put my arm around Yunichi's shoulders; Akira did the same; we mumbled yoroshiku. Yunichi's face had got outright maroon; he went toward the toilets but couldn't make it, so Akira helped him up; but Yunichi shaped up, did something good there, and came back on his own, now in a better state of balance than Akira and I were.

Then all three of us, taking turns, had persuaded the round lady to drink some with us, too. Kumiko was her name, Big Kumiko. With a smile on her moon-face, her eyes became just narrow slits, and even the slits emanated cheerfulness, and she downed the little cups so fast that we noticed, with respect. The only words heard were *domo, dozo, arigato,* and *yoroshiku,* till Akira started to sing "Akatombo," an old folk favorite about a red dragonfly, the tune that garbage collectors' trucks play to announce their arrival. He even acted out the parts. Yunichi tried hard to remember a song from his childhood. A nice tune, but he only hummed most of it, forgetting the refrain. My song, "My Darling Clementine," was really pitiful, since I had to make up some of the words just to carry the tune. But by then our hearts were wide open.

It was then that Yunichi had tilted too much to one side again and Kumiko-san had decided we needed something to eat. She hollered: "*Natsuko-chan!*"—but then changed her mind and rushed to the kitchen. Soon she was back with four little trays of laquered wood piled with steaming mushrooms.

"*Maitake!*" Yunichi had regained his balance in an instant. "Delicious. *Oishii, oishii,*" the poet said. "You know maitake?" he asked.

"Don't know. Looks like slices of coral. But smells good," I said.

"*M-a-i*—it means 'to dance.' Know why the name maitake?"

"No. And I wondered."

"Out of happiness one wants to dance—*mai*—when one finds *maitake* in the forest," Yunichi explained. "They are best sautéed in oil and sake with a dash of soy sauce. *Oishii.* Delicious!" Still excited, Yunichi had started to explain; he lumbered to stand up and demonstrate the dance—*mai.* This, Akira and I had prevented just in time. *Maitake* was a treat of indescribably delicate, unpronounced flavor.

"You are the greatest cook in Kamikawa, perhaps, Kumiko-san," I complimented our friend.

"Thank you, thank you teacher, *sensei,*" she bowed, using the most honorable title she could think of. "But it was made by *Natsuko-chan,* my daughter." All three of us, in surprising synchrony, had expressed an urgent desire to meet Natsuko-san, Kumiko's daughter. "*Natsuko-chan!*" roared Kumiko in the direction of the kitchen.

Silence engulfed the room. I folded my legs back into an orderly crossed position. Yunichi combed his long hair with his fingers, and Akira wiped the sweat off his brows and raised the knot of his tie a couple of inches. "*Hi, so deska, hi, so desu, ne,*" he mumbled to himself, then stopped and opened his mouth.

Natsuko had appeared in front of us as if from nowhere and bowed with a smile so shy I had become almost sober. Despite her youth, the greatest attribute of a woman, one could suspect a resemblance to her mother. But when her eyes disappeared with the smile, I was certain of their relationship. She had a round face, a village face with good cheekbones that needed no cosmetics to radiate health. Her hair was braided into two jet-black, eel-like ponytails (something unacceptable in Tokyo), my all-time favorite hairdo, because my sweetheart at home wears it that way when we go skiing.

She accepted a place by our table, and we took turns with what we were sure were jokes and witticisms. I wanted desperately to be popular, so I tried some of the *geisha* lingo I had learned, assuming it would sound ridiculous and therefore entertaining from the mouth of a male—and a foreigner to boot. She laughed, indeed, when I asked for the salt not using "*o-shio*" but the geishas' "*nami no hana*"—which means "blossom of the wave." The laughter I was rewarded with came from under the palm covering her mouth. Then I ran out of words.

Kumiko and Natsuko exchanged a short animated dialogue that ended, from what I understood, with victory for the mother: Natsuko-san would sing to us in real English. There was a brand new karioke set on the bar, and the girl put a tape in it. She had an American flag patch on her jeans, sewed onto the left half of her ample (and I mean ample) bottom. (Sewed there with good intentions, no doubt, in the spirit of yoroshiku.) She took the microphone, and with the other hand she swung one of her ponytails onto the front of her shoulder; then she bowed to us. Her mother sank down to join us again on our sake-soaked *tatami* mat. When the background music started to pour out of the karioke speakers, we froze, motionless.

"You are my sunshine, my only sunshine," she'd sung the old favorite. And when she sang it, she looked straight into my eyes. "You are my sunshine, my only . . ." she'd sung again the refrain, looking straight into my open heart, I swear, and she'd smiled that smile at me as she sang it, too, that enormous smile with no eyes, and almost perfect teeth, with only one incisor out of place, and with those two black beautiful eels flowing from her scalp like ponytails.

I'd thought, *this must be the corniest performance ever witnessed,* and after the second chorus I was embarrassed a little, I remember that. But in about the middle of the song I felt something tightening in my gut, and felt a strange feeling in my heart already softened by the sake and yoroshiku. It took maybe another minute or so for me to fall in love with her. I loved her with abandon by the time she'd finished telling me that I was her only sunshine, and I believed every word.

When Natsuko switched the karioke off, she had looked at me again, sideways, with a little smile—and she was gone. Yunichi was leaning too much to one side again. Akira's head had found a wet place between the sake cups. And I was in love. We had ended in bad shape, with no perspective.

Of the way home I remember only wading through the ice-cold creek, carrying Yunichi on my back, his thumb in my right eye. From up there he had recited his instant haiku:

> Spring ice-flows chiming
> to wake up and cheer the buds
> of weeping willow.

For this verse of beauty I would have carried him all night. Maybe I did. There is a blank in my memory.

The train arrived in Kyoto on time, as always. I stumbled out and found myself on the platform, towering over a crowd of schoolchildren with identical faces. It seemed that half of them were watching my expression, that of a lost pilgrim.

Soon I found a "business hotel," a category known for reasonable rates and the tiniest of rooms, even by Japanese and submarine standards. My allowance had been calculated in such a way that it excluded any possibility of other types of accommodation (and excluded boozing in some mountain village with my local pals). My assignment was spelled out clearly: get photographs of people (two-thirds), the countryside, and shrines (one-third). Eighty percent on colored slides, the rest black-and-white prints. Get "special interest": religious activities, festivals, shrines, and priests. That is what *Minnesota Magazine* paid for, half in advance.

I knew I had to get organized, since Kyoto was my last stop, and I had not done too well, so far. So I prepared the gear and films in the evening and set the alarm clock for seven. For the famous stone garden in the Zen monastery I wanted the low sun of early morning with its long shadows. There was a small *shinto* shrine in the back of my hotel.

So I went out and sat near the *tori* gate, to calm down and breathe a little before going to bed. It was a windless night; the temperature was benign. A peaceful evening.

I heard the music of a *shamisen* seeping from the shrine. The tune seemed like gossamer strings reaching softly between the black needles of a red pine to the moon. The moon sank slowly out of sight—and when it vanished, the shamisen became mute. Then only the shrieks of Hondas could be heard from under the fluorescent street lights.

In bed I wondered if, indeed, the shamisen, *"neko,"* was made of the hide of a virgin cat, so that the nipples would still be closed and tiny. Falling asleep I did not want to anticipate possible difficulties with tomorrow's shoot—the last one in this country that I liked so much, now, after Kamikawa.

I pushed the release on the Hasselblad camera for the first time at exactly a quarter to eight. The Zen Buddhist monastery was a quiet place, this early in the morning, the misty serenity of its garden still undisturbed by eager tourists. I worked from a walkway around the stone garden, getting the shots at angles and with lighting that enhanced its secret beauty. Secret for me, since my understanding of Zen was almost nonexistent. Little did I know that this would improve shortly when I noticed a young monk scuttling in my direction.

He was a tall fellow, for a Japanese, clad in a black robe with wide sleeves, wooden *gettas* on his feet over white socks with separate big toes. He dragged his feet, making a shuffling sound. He was interested in my photographic undertaking, because he slowed down on approach. *"Ohio gozaimasu,"* I greeted him politely. He stopped and answered my greeting with a bow.

If ever there was an ascetic-looking follower of Zen, this monk was the prototype. His paleness was striking; the color of his clean-shaven skull did not differ from the color of his cheeks. In the Orient, the most prized of jades is "mutton-fat jade." Off-white with a touch of grey, it is slightly translucent, and when polished the surface acquires a sheen that does not glisten but looks like living matter that has died. His face was carved out of such stuff. It had not seen a summer beach at Nihonkai—ever.

He did not have slanted eyes; the Asian epicanthus was barely suggested, and his lips were thin. My mother would have said he didn't look too healthy and would suggest a diet of Czech dumplings, fat roast pork and sauerkraut, and for dessert a heap of noon-time sunshine, holes in the ozone notwithstanding. Through my mind an image flashed of the girl in Kamikawa singing about sunshine, and my heart constricted for a few seconds. The monk constructed a smile, and we conversed as long as my limited *Nihongo* lasted. I told him how impressed I was with the monastery and the garden.

"Would you like to observe more? To see inside the monastery?" he asked, after a while.

"Very much. Very much, thank you," I said, pleased. I was finished photographing the garden. I packed up in a hurry and followed him through the *shoji* screen he had opened with the usual care Japanese pay to their delicate screens. He closed the screen door behind us with a clap. If only I could take his photograph—that would top this shoot! But I would not dare.

The room was of a good size, about fifteen tatami mats large. Walls and posts were of nicely aged cedar. The posts were made of slender tree trunks off which only the bark had been carefully peeled, revealing the natural imperfections and thus fitting perfectly into the stark non-architecture of the chamber. There was no furniture there, only a rack holding several paddle-like wooden instruments that looked pretty much like cricket bats. Zen cricket?

"This is our hall for meditation," the monk interrupted the silence. "We sit here in a special position, right here along the wall," he pointed.

"*Ah, so desu ne!* The position of lotus? Is that it?" I asked.

"Would you like to try it?" he surprised me. This was actually the first time he had talked looking directly into my face.

"Thank you; I would like to try it. *Suki desu*," I said, and bowed slightly to his bowing. "And what are these paddles for? Those things here?"

"Ah—do not worry, please. These are instruments the teacher, *sensei*, uses."

"Uses for what?" I insisted.

"When the disciple fails to maintain the correct position with a straight and upright back, he is hit with the paddle. Then he corrects the position."

Oh, shit, I thought. *I bet he does.*

"Please, sit down here." He pointed to the mat in front of us. We were sitting close to each other, I facing the wall, my friend facing me. I tried, with some success, the infamous lotus posture, with legs cross-contorted painfully, my hands lying on my thighs and my back straightened as much as I could. He looked at me with concentrated eyes and nodded with approval. I was grateful, now, to benefit from

Yoroshiku   69

countless hours of sitting cross-legged in many a bar, *geisha* house, and immoral "Members Club" all over this country.

The monk's hand touched the nape of my neck, and slowly his palm slid down along my spine to my tailbone. (Just checking.) "Very correct," he said. I was proud, a little. My first time doing the Zen thing—and I am approved by a real pro. But my cheer was premature; a frown crossed the otherwise expressionless face of my sensei, my newfound teacher. He fixed his eyes on my belly, and a gesture of his hand suggested to me to pull it in more. More!

Not satisfied with my sincere effort, he laid his palm right under my rib-cage and pushed. I tried my best. But that was not enough; his hand descended, very slowly, to the area of my belly button, exerting a moderate pressure. Then it descended lower, and finally, lowest. There it remained. He'd got me by the balls!

I did not move, successfully suppressing the simple reflex of aggression in my right fist. In my brain, cells and neuronal connections went into mental overdrive. Photography! I removed his hand slowly and stood up. I stretched, to prevent multiple muscle spasms after my lotus position. I smiled at him, and asked him to stand up and position himself next to the paper screen, through which light softly penetrated from outside. No, he cannot object, now.

I made the first photograph paying attention to proper exposure and depth of field. I changed lenses, shot a few more, and went outside and finished the roll, photographing my friend in front of varied and always beautiful backgrounds. The monk's face remained expressionless, as I would want it; thus I knew these pictures would be the best from my Japanese assignment. A most pleasurable assignment, in a country I liked much and had started to understand just a tiny, tiny bit. At the end I started to feel a little guilty. Then more guilt and no sympathy for myself, at all. I tortured the guy.

"*Arigato*," I said, and bowed to him. "*Arigato gozaimasu. Arigato gozaimashta. Domo, arigato gaozaimashta.*" I ascended the scale of politeness in thanking him, and my uneasiness went partly away. I turned around and hurried straight to the Golden Pavilion Bar and ordered Suntory whisky with water. What else should I have done?

The first one I drank for *yoroshiku*, to my Zen friend. I wanted him to sit with me now, to make up to him; I needed a stiff one. The next one I drank to her. Natsuko was her name, Natsuko-chan. I closed my eyes and could see her face, her smile, as if she said to me: "My sunshine, look—no eyes!" I had polished off another Suntory, lifting the tumbler just to *yoroshiku*. To *yoroshiku*!

It was still early in the day; this must be the last drink for me. I started to feel the sadness of a traveler who has reached his destination, celebrated his achievement, and then ended the celebration, alone.

I stood up. The familiar melody of "Akatombo" reached me from the street outside. The garbage collector's truck was announcing its arrival.

Ladies of the Brussels Night

On dévient moral des qu'on est malheureux.
(As soon as one is unhappy one becomes moral.)
Marcel Proust

As soon as one becomes moral one becomes a moralist.
(Tak se z něj stal moralista, nabubřelej, věc to jistá.)
Jára Červenků

Mixing colors makes, sometimes, unexpected hues; a few drops of black paint in the white brightens the white whiter. A bucket of black night over the beige haze of city lights made the sky above the horizon glow the color of an old-fashioned dusty rose. The stretched noodle of the autobahn, thinned in the distance into a hair by the rules of perspective, led directly into the center of the rosy horizon. Their SKODA, the asthmatic four-cyclinder "FAVORITE," did the best that Czech engineering allowed, in the right lane. They had been driving all day, and finally, the sky in front of them announced the city of their destination, Brussels.

The glow brought a memory from what seemed to be prehistoric times. When Tara was little she used to spend a couple of weeks in grandmother's house in Kladno every summer. That city has been known for the largest steel plant and smelters in Czechoslovakia. And everybody knew it was the ugliest town in the country, urban refuse by any standards except those of a little girl with ponytails at Granny's house. Tara used to love everything about Kladno, including the

73

unpaved, muddy streets where one could scrape the butter-smooth ochre clay from the deepest rut, and the skeleton-like acacias that were dwarfed nicely by acid rains to climbable size, and under them the prematurely ancient men and women wilted into incredible bends, who either smiled at you or threatened to tell Grandma; and the rowdy packs of kids with their homemade carts, and slingshots, and dolls with heads made of old stockings with sewed-on buttons for eyes.

If pure accidents, such as the fight with Kaja Blaha from Krocehlavy or perhaps a broken window, or a fence climbed, or an exclamation in foul language, had not been reported to Grandma by the end of the day, and if Tara had already washed her hands and neck without being reminded a hundred times, she could be sure of a special reward. After darkness fell and the cuckoo clock in the kitchen announced bedtime, Grandma would take her hand and lead her to the bedroom, switch off the lights, push back the drapes, and put a stool under the window. Tara would climb on it, press her nose on the windowpane, and wait. Always, they waited in silence as if even a whisper could prevent the magic from happening. Tara would peer into the darkness, trying to make out the concentration of flickering dots of light outlining the steel plant and smelters in the far distance.

Then the magic would happen, without warning: a volcanic eruption on a South Seas Island on a tropical midnight! A faintly pink halo appeared over the plant, grew bigger and brighter and all the horizon and all the sky would turn rosy, then change to crimson crinoline covering the city, without a sound. It lasted and lasted, then contracted, died, gave way to foggy darkness again. In the steel plant they had opened the smelting tower and let the man-made lava flow out. But Tara did not want to know that. She witnessed a volcano erupting, raging forest fires, hell, battlefields—depending on the daydream. That had been three decades ago.

"Tara, you are crossing the line again," her husband, Pepa, sighed from the passenger seat. "And you're going too fast!"

"Yeah." Their SKODA was braving the maximum RPMs she could muster and still machines with Belgian and German license plates passed them as if they were parked. The car was tired, and they were tired. The rosy sky over the horizon brought back Tara's memories but did not generate nostalgia or dreams of romance. The only dream she had was a vision of a shower and a bed. It was a realistic hope, finally.

"It must be Brussels under that sky. It better be," Tara said.

"Yes, you might be right. It's almost midnight." Pepa's throat felt like a drainage pipe.

"How's ma baby doing?"

Pepa leaned by her side and looked at the back seat. His face returned with a smile. "Sleeping. Can see just his hair from under the blanket. He doesn't mind nothing. And we are on the way for about... let me see... sixteen hours. Sixteen!" He stretched. "Do you want coffee, Tara? There might be some left in the thermos."

"No, thanks, we should be there soon. Maybe an hour?" She felt her back aching, neck stiffened, beat. "I was thinking" she said while another Mercedes jetted by, doing well over a hundred miles an hour.

"Did you see *that*?" Pepa interjected with an admiring accent on "that."

"I was thinking. We just can't knock on Lejeunes' door in the middle of the night, drag them out of bed. What do you say?" Tara said.

"Crossed my mind too."

"So?"

"So, we'll try to find a place to shack in," Pepa said. "There must be some small hotels around the Gran' Place. I remember, vaguely."

They had crossed all of Germany, stopping just for minutes at a time, and were nearing their limit of endurance. *That is how their vacations abroad had always started, always,* Tara thought. This time the plan was to stay for a few days in Brussels with their friends, the Lejeunes, and then, together with them, go to Westende, to the beach, cooking mussels, fishing on Lejeunes' boat, doing nothing, talking about everything, a lot.

Tara tilted the mirror to see the blond tuft of hair on the back seat. *His coloring takes after mine,* she thought. *At his five years it radiates like platinum, even in the twilight. And his eyes are Scandinavian blue, to match the hair.* She wondered if they would turn khaki with age, like hers. In those five years he had grown like a bamboo shoot. Amazing, from a zygote to such a precious kid! She wished he wouldn't change so fast, though, lose his sunny disposition, the smile that doesn't leave him even in sleep, the eagerness and abandon in anything he does. He has been a good traveler too. He had to be. She tilted the mirror back. They were past the suburbs, now, in the city, still on the throughway.

"Tara, I would take the first exit, and then we might ask somebody."

It had been two years since they last visited here. Lejeunes took them around the town, this Eurocapital. They visited the sites, the old theater quarter, Petit Rue des Bouchers where every house is a restaurant, Gran' Place, the fairy-tale square. In the Royal Museum they marveled at the imagination of home-boy Magritte, the magician of realistic surreal; they drove through the red-lighted street of sins;

they took part in the photographing orgy at the tourists' favorite—Manneken Pis, the eternally pissing statue of an angelic youngster. Not to speak of churches.

Maybe I can get a position-reading, direction, at some of the "orientation points," she thought, *maybe the pissing kid statue, or something.* "We are lost, Pepa. I don't have a clue where we are now." Then the sprawling Gare du Nord appeared in front of them, lighted like an amusement park.

"Hey, I remember this train station! We are not far from the Centre." Pepa woke up from his dormancy. "There are always a few hotels near a station."

She turned into the first side street, drove up, turned the corner, entered another street—but nothing. No hotel sign, nobody on the street, deserted. The watch said one-forty. When she spotted a man sauntering with uncertain gait in a winding track, she stopped the car. "Pepa," she said, and pointed to the walker. From the backseat Alex mumbled something about pulling the fish in, his sleep disturbed by the sudden absence of the engine's rumble.

Pepa stumbled out of the car, crossed the street, and surprised the lonely walker. Thick vapors engulfed him: Stella Artois, the most popular of local brews, Pepa was certain. "Bon soir. I am wondering if you might know, by chance, about a hotel around here, nearby?"

The man steadied himself on a lamppost: "Huh?" Pepa repeated his query in three simple words. The man scratched his eyebrow and put on a frown of seriousness: "Yeah, you are in luck. That way." He detached himself from the lamp, wavered in the night wind drafting down the street, and pointed out a general direction in a sweep. "Just turn the corner over there. You'll see many hotels. Many." His benumbed tongue articulated with an effort. Then he shuffled backwards, emitting strange sounds, watching Pepa crossing the street back to the car.

There were many hotels in the street behind the corner, many. One next to another, small hotels announced their hospitality in bright red neon signs. There was nobody walking the street at this late hour to enjoy the celebratory lighting, which contrasted so pleasantly with the grimness of the streets they had just left. A shower and a sprawling bed appeared imminent, to Tara and Pepa, and they stopped in front of the first hotel on the right.

The door was locked. Pepa rang, waited, rang again. His resignation to fatigue changed to a furious determination to break in. Then a key rattled in the lock, the door moved, and in the fissure a man appeared. His waxy face did not beam with joy under the disheveled remnants of colorless hair; his expression, wordlessly, accused them of dragging him from a pleasant dream.

Pepa apologized and begged him for a room: "Nous voudrions une chambre," adding the "S'il vous plaît" with as much humility as he could manage. The old man appeared not to understand. "We have been driving eighteen hours," (he exaggerated by two) "across all of Germany. What shall we do?"

"You've got an accent," the man said after a while, his face showing signs of involvement, which Pepa translated as "hope."

"Yes, we are Czechs, from Prague."

The man lighted up in an instant, opened the door, and motioned Pepa in. He actually smiled. "Karlsbad, Karlovy Vary!" He raised his arm as if lifting an object on his open palm. "I have spent half of my life shuttling between here and Karlsbad. Jak se mas? Nazdar, kamarade!"

Pepa knew they'd found shelter. With Tara in the car, surely anxious to know what was happening, he listened to this kind man with his impatience concealed. It was an abbreviated, ten-minute story, how the man used to be a porcelain salesman, buying china in Czechoslovakia and importing it to Belgium and Holland, and how he had one mistress and one serious girlfriend in Karlsbad for all those years, both wonderful and, in spite of them, how he still saved money to buy this place for retirement.

In the time-honored Gallic gesture the man puckered his lips, inflated one cheek, blew out the air while shaking his hand from the wrist as if it was burnt. "Sorry, sorry, taking your time like that! You must be fatigué." He gave a key to Pepa and pointed to a circular staircase. "Number two. You'll find it quiet. And clean." Then he descended down to somewhere.

Tara dragged the army-surplus duffel bag and Pepa carried Alex, still asleep, upstairs. Entering their room, Tara dropped the bag and Pepa tightened his hold on Alex, speechless. They surveyed the chamber: blood-red flutter-drapes covered one wall from the ceiling to the floor. A mirrored dresser was decorated by a vase with artificial flowers in colors never seen in nature, not even on the shore of the Amazon. Two cardinal-red plastic chairs, a gold and red painted imitation-antique almara, the floor covered with an obviously fake Isphahan, its crimson mercifully worn down. The most prominent structure, which took up a quarter of the floor space, was an airport of a fourposter bed. "Wow!" they said, shaking their heads.

After a symbolic wash-up in a porcelain washbasin they took off the red bedspread, speedily, and collapsed onto the fluffy heaven without much comment, laying Alex between them. "Good night."

"Night."

But the last word heard in the red chamber was "Unbelievable!" Tara pointed above their communal bed. Pepa looked up to see all three of them in a large mirror attached on the ceiling above the bed. Then the Sandman blurred the mirror with a puff of sand, bringing dreams to the weary travelers.

After six hours of blissful unconsciousness, Tara's hand touched only a vacant space between her and Pepa. She opened her eyes. The narrow sheet of light penetrating between the gory drapes confirmed that Alex was missing. She sat up and scanned the room. He was gone. It took a hurried minute to put on jeans, a sweater over her naked torso, and shoes sans socks. She shook Pepa: "Alex's gone! I am running to check outside." Pepa's eyes opened wide but remained dead, absent, his stupor still deep.

Tara ran down the stairs holding onto the banister with one hand, combing her hair with the fingers of the other. At the bottom of the staircase there was a short, dark corridor lighted by a naked bulb of low voltage. The corridor led to a room flooded with golden light, the light one feels one can almost touch, like in Vermeer's paintings or Sudek's photographs. *"Belichtung ist alles,"* she would agree with the German photographer. It was an illumination that makes common things glow as if coated with wildflower honey. It poured in from a large window, set from the floor almost to the ceiling, facing the street full of the morning sun. There, Alex took part in a scene which halted Tara's steps. "Alex," she said quietly.

"Hi ma!" He turned his head, donated a smile, and turned away again. It took a second. At least half of the room was taken up by a bar. Behind the bar was the usual wall of shelves with liquors and distillates. One of the barstools was occupied by an impressive specimen of a female.

Tara noticed her crossed legs of athletic build which the leopard-patterned leotard hugged tightly, to be admired in their entirety. The second thing she noticed was the ease and comfort of her son sitting on the woman's lap, pushed slightly to one side by her chest, the size of which would be difficult to describe believably. It was revealed to the maximum possible extent. The lady was holding Alex around his tiny shoulders with one hand; her second hand was lifting a glass of what looked like orange juice to Alex's mouth.

A second girl was coming from behind the bar carrying a tray of pastry. She gave Tara a surprised look but, in an instant, concentrated on arranging the sweets in front of Alex. She wore a metallic microskirt, black net stockings on swift-runner's legs, and a top made of a small piece of leather constructed to enhance her abyss-deep cleavage. The most remarkable feature was her strawberry hair, ripe strawberry, forming a tower of luxuriant curls. She petted Alex's scalp of platinum and in hushed, machine-gun French promoted her pastries. Both girls chuckled when the kid told them, in Czech, that he would eat it all.

"He said, he likes everything," Tara translated and stepped farther into the room. Two steps.

"Is your boy?" the leopard-leotarded lady asked in a stark voice.

"Yes, he is. We have to leave soon." The amusement disappeared from the girls' faces.

"I don't wanna, Mom." He did not turn around; his voice was muted by the Belgian pastry. Both girls nodded in his support, understanding the meaning without knowing his foreign words.

Tara noticed the third girl, who sat, motionless, on a chair by the window. She had round eyes which gave her face an expression of wonder because the eyelids did not cover even a part of the iris: the eyes of a kid looking at a lighted Christmas tree. They did not leave Alex for a second. The head of that girl was completely shaved. Tara nodded at her, but remained unseen.

Tara looked out the window across the street. The houses were narrow, none wider than three lengths of a car. In each house there was a large picture window, elevated just a few feet above the sidewalk. In each of the windows there was a chair or two, and on the chairs sat living females, like mannequins, in scant clothing of pastel or fluorescent hues.

She knew this street! Two years ago, Lucien Lejeune had driven Pepa and her around the town, showed them the tourists' sites and included this street because it was *"très intéressant. N'est-çe pas?"* She remembered her reaction of disgust as well: yes, it was *très intéressant*, as *intéressant* as a liquidation sale. She recalled Pepa's remarks, too. Embarrassing. He wanted to drive slower and babbled something about the oldest, honorable profession in the world, giggling like an idiot. She was sure she remembered this place.

The girl with the shaved head and the eyes watched the miracle of Alex intently, as he spilled the juice, which the strawberry-haired girl gently, carefully wiped off his chin.

"We really have to go, Alex. Alex, dear!" The leopard-leotarded lady put him down on the floor as one would lower an alabaster statue of great value. Alex extended his arm and touched the black net stocking of the strawberry lady. She smiled at him. She bent down, holding her breasts in place with one hand, smoothing Alex's hair with the other.

"You have slept here?" The Leopard turned to Tara. "In this house?"

"Oui, we did. My husband waits upstairs," Tara said. The girls looked at her, as if not understanding. Only the one with the shaved head still did not take her eyes off Alex. He wandered to her, to the window.

"May I ask something?" Tara took courage. There was no response, just questioning stares. "I was wondering, why did the lady by the window shave her hair? It is quite unusual, isn't it?"

Strawberry said: "Her best friend lost her hair after chemo. Chemotherapy, you know? So she shaved, too. Sympathy."

"I understand. How unhappy she must have been, about her friend."

"Oh no, she wasn't. That's how life is," Strawbery said, with a hardened expression "but she cried a lot; she cried."

"Most of the customers want her just to hold them now. Just that, you know?" Leopard came to life, a little, turned to her Strawberry friend. "The older ones."

"They want me to do the same." Strawberry told her. "Some of the older guys, married mecs, they want just to be held. Has nothing to do with hair. And you know it."

"Yeah, they need that, ç'est vrai. Has nothing to do with the haircut." Leopard turned to Tara. "You married, aren't you?"

Tara nodded.

"No fucky-fucky pas, just to be held they want. *Vous comprenez? Pige?*" She giggled.

Tara felt uneasy, tight in her chest—*this conversation is not very good*, she thought. She did not know what to say, if anything.

"But you have a very handsome boy. Nice *bebe*," said Strawberry, the smile melting her painted face.

"*Merci bien, merci.* You took good care of him," Tara said, grateful for the change of topic. She forced a short laugh: "You would spoil him rotten. With those sweets, I mean," she added very quickly. "But we must be on the way now." She took the sticky hand of Alex. "Thanks, again. So kind of you."

The room became very silent then. Alex followed Tara with his head turned back, waving at the girls in a child's way, just with his fingers.

In their room Pepa was dressed, ready to go. "Where was he? Is he all right?" he asked about Alex. Tara looked at her husband. He has shaved, had combed his hair and packed their things, even tidied the bed, sort of. He looked good. For his age he looked very good. She should hug him, hold him, she should. Just hold him. She looked at the bed, with the mirror above it. She took a deep breath. She had a strange thought. How about not just holding him. Wouldn't it be something? The enormous bed, the mirror and all? But what to do with Alex? She took another deep breath and swallowed. She felt heat in her cheeks.

"You have slept in a whorehouse, Pepa." She tried to sound matter-of-fact. Pepa put down the bag, stiffened, and spread his arms, staring at Tara without words, his forehead in a wrinkled frown.

"Where did you get this idea? I don't want to talk about anything like that, now. I mean—let's go, let's get going, Tara!" Pepa stuttered and moved to the door.

That despicable lowlife; he certainly has been in a whorehouse, somewhere. I know it. Look at him! She would like to kiss him for how worried he looks. He has been good to her and to Alex, always, a good friend, too, that lowlife. She really loves the guy—later, she'll hug him, later.

"Pepa, I am telling you, this place is a bordello, brothel, house of ill repute, whatever. Look around!"

Pepa sighed as if relieved and looked around, obediently. "I'll be damned," he said. "I'll be damned." He managed a smile. His relief showed plainly.

Tara told him about Alex and the ladies downstairs, about the window to the street. "Do you remember? Two years ago we drove through here with Lucien?"

Pepa laughed. Alex looked at him and laughed, too. They went downstairs and Pepa paid the ex-porcelain-salesman a price obviously discounted (since no special services were rendered and the bed provided had been uninhabited). They got into their car parked in front of the house. It started after a series of coughs.

Alex knelt on the back seat, peering out of the car. "Bye, bye. Bye," he was shouting. All three girls stood behind the large picture window, waving; even the motionless one without hair raised her hand. The window blurred their images, took off their colors, the window's tempered thickness giving it strength exceeding the strength of prison iron bars and seven locks, making it impenetrable.

They drove the length of the street. Alex was waving at all the large windows with beautiful ladies. Then they turned the corner. The displays in the large windows changed with an abruptness which surprised them both and prevented any comment. Ladies were replaced by grilled quails, cheeses the size of a wheel, miniature castles of chocolate, marinated octopi. The rows of *charcuteries, brasseries, boulangeries,* and *pâtisseries* announced the domain of *citoyen moral,* whose chief permissible celebration of life was a pleasurable way of feeding.

"We should get something small to eat. Or at least a coffee, and milk for the boy." Pepa said, slowing down, looking for a café or brasserie.

"That house, the 'hotel' where we slept tonight—was number three, I think. Wasn't it?" Tara said. "Did you notice the name of that street?"

Pepa looked at her for a long time, considering he was driving in traffic. "Tara! Don't even think about that! Tara, I know you."

"What do you mean?"

"What do I mean? I mean: don't even think about taking Alex back to that house, to those girls, there! Jesus Christ, Tara."

"Ma, can you take me back to those girls? Please," Alex whined from the back seat. Pepa held back a smile with an effort. Always, he had admired her "compassion for the sediment"; that's what he called it. Compassion for those lacking good fortune. That's what he admired about her.

They drove in silence. It looked like an optimistic day in the making; the sun was high already. Pepa placed his fingertips on Tara's cheek, then laid his hand on her thigh and squeezed gently. He shook his head with a small smile on his face, looking straight ahead.

Tara seemed to watch the road, too. Her thoughts were too crowded, louder than the morning traffic rushing by, louder than the roar of the moral city around them. She thought about Strawberry and Leopard and the Shaved one, about the world she had always imagined as being carnival or carnivore, but glimpsing into it she had found it might not be either. About the world she had left just minutes ago, the world which would not leave her.

The second day of their stay with Lejeunes, Tara and Alex said they were going shopping. They returned very late for lunch. They'd got lost in town, she explained, trying to look believable. They couldn't find a taxi, she said. Pepa didn't ask anything. She looked happy, radiant. She smiled at him, and he smiled at her, silently, knowing.

On Brainwaves of Memory

What beastly incidents our memories insist on cherishing.
                                                    Eugene O'Neill

Most roofers do it. When they finish a copper roof, they pee on it to start the chemical reaction. The persimmon gloss is speed-aged to the green-grey malachite of baroque bronze. To generate a sufficient volume of urine, the roofer drinks a gallon of beer and gets very happy and uncertain in his balance. (A case is known of a plastered roofing specialist who lost his footing on the steep roof of the St. Ludmila Cathedral and slid in the direction of the two-hundred-foot drop, only to be arrested in his fall by the statue of a watchful gargoyle. Lying in the gutter, he fell asleep instantly, complicating his rescue by a special unit of mountain climbers.)

Old sandstone and marble buildings of historical significance can be aged nicely, too, not by urine but by acid rain, noxious fumes, and deposits of dust. But a building of no historical significance, like the high school in Prague-6, would not weather well, because it was a contemporary structure. At least we thought of it as modern, since the proportion of glass to stucco on its facade favored glass. Dust and grime from the traffic below has deposited a makeup of dejection and fatigue on its face, saddest on a sunny day. It seemed to match the expression of students leaving the open sky and their partial liberty for its torture chambers of dead languages and calculus.

I remember, in Shakespeare's words, "creeping like snail unwillingly to school," then slowing down to a standstill in front of that building. There, I used to hope to sight a friend who would help me through the glass door of the entrance. Anyone of our Group, as we called ourselves, would do. Pepik Pycha might shuffle from up the street from Hanspaulka.

Pepik had gained notoriety for his inimitable laugh, which roared with well-separated syllables, "ha - ha," often in the middle of a teacher's monologue, and always propping up his jokes. He knew hundreds of disgusting jokes without ever writing any down—such was the memory of Pepik Pycha. His grades were far less than mediocre, because of his feeble memory (he said). After three years of compulsory Russian language, when everybody was reading Russian classics, Pepik still confused the capital letters of the Cyrillic alphabet.

Lubos Hanzlik might approach from up the hill too. We admired the many pockets of his U.S. Army jacket, the army cap, and the Camels he offered to anyone in the Group but to nobody else. He boasted a C in Morals and Behavior, for his disturbances and cheekiness. His flunking of Art was admired as a unique achievement. It was hard to understand because his creations resembled so closely the paintings of "primitives" much valued by galleries in those times of socialist realism. Lubos was a big guy but not a pretty boy. These physical attributes of fierceness had not made him less popular, because they helped him to emanate confidence. He had grown to a great height in spite of efforts by his mother, who used to give him cigarettes in his preadolescence in an attempt to stunt his growth.

I could wait a few minutes for the next tram No. 24, carrying Kaja Fot. He was the handsome one of the Group, whose unprovable stories of his amorous adventures we wished to believe, because they gave us hope. His carefully staged arrogance endeared him to some of his peers but failed to impress any teacher. This contributed to his abysmal grades.

Latin class started with the same ritual, always, without variation. When that relic of Austrian monarchy, the bearded Professor Kramar, entered the classroom following his own beerbelly, everybody stood up, and in one voice we had to greet him in Latin: "*Salve domine professor!*" Without giving us a glance, Kramar marched to his desk. He turned to the class—"*Salvete discipuli!*"—and then motioned us to sit down with a gesture which might have been confused with the signal for an execution.

"Fot!" Professor then exclaimed, and Kaja Fot stood up. Kramar asked him the meaning of a Latin word, which Kaja, unfailingly, did not know. "F!" roared the old man, and recorded the failing grade in his classbook. And then class began. Every day this minidrama started our Latin education, and it soon elevated Fot to the respectable status of somebody notorious and remarkable, of an admirably strong will. So he became one of the Group, where these were the most appreciated attributes of a man in his teen years of burrowing acne and perpetual longing for a lay.

The power of scholastic failure was valued, then. It was an expression of dissent, of revolt against the authority and Communistic idiocy of the spineless, and against the political chameleonization of our poor teachers. But what mattered to us the most was that these demonstrative failures increased one's stature in many a misty eye of a well-endowed female schoolmate.

Kaja Fot emerged from tram No. 24 just before I entered the building. I waited for him, and we greeted each other mutely, just with our eyes. "Again!" he said, and elongated his face.

"Shit," I said, and we entered.

"Today, I'll walk Jana Volavkova home from school," Kaja remarked, waiting for my comment.

"I don't know, man. Remember last week? When she gave you a fat lip after you praised the bulges in her sweater?"

"Yeah. It hurt. She plays tennis, man. She's some piece of work."

"That movie, yesterday. Incredible!" I changed the topic. Yesterday we'd had to attend a Russian movie about "heroes of socialist work," coal miners, who had fulfilled their Five Year Plan in four. Attendance was compulsory, and headcounts had been made by teachers who watched vigilantly for anybody who might laugh. Any loud sighs of admiration were recorded, too, as provocations.

"Torture, bore!" Kaja tilted his head backward and howled, not unlike a wolf. People around us paid attention; some stopped. Just in time we entered the classroom, where we survived till noon, each hovering over our private dreamscapes.

During the noon break we had to "circulate," walk the school's corridors without stopping. Our Group of four was together, as usual, talking in short utterances about yesterday's movie, enjoying the felicities of the crudest possible expressions. Jana Volavkova passed by us during the circulation, in her new pink sweater. It might have been the view of what the sweater tried to conceal that impressed Kaja Fot again. He dropped to his knees by the wall of the hallway and, using an imaginary pick, he started to imitate the digging of a Russian miner, the hero of socialist work, from yesterday's flick. Within seconds Pepik Pycha, Lubos Hanzlik, and I, the Group, were on our knees toiling in the mine shaft with dramatic gestures and faces distorted by fatigue, barely bearable.

Suddenly, the crowed around us dispersed. There, in the vacant space, stood Professor Konecna, Party Member and terrorist, feared by everybody in the school with the exception of the janitor-doorman Pudlak, who was an informer for the Czech KGB. Like an overweight angel of death, she loomed over us, recording our names. Then she disappeared, evaporated without comment. We knew that the trouble ahead would be of the serious kind.

In a couple of days each one of us "miners" was informed by a letter of stark sentences that we would spend one month "shock-working," harvesting the famous red Semsch hops. It is dirty slavery that includes sleeping in sex-segregated barns, eating tripe soup, and being harassed by moronic villagers with sadistic inclinations. The verdict was final and did not allow for any exceptions—save illness. This exception had to be discussed.

After the last lecture that day, the convicts in the Group did not leave the classroom. We sat in a circle on the desks, heads together. Of the other students, only Josh Osten stayed, writing something, in the front row. Osten was a good fellow who could be trusted, for he too was prone to rebellion and rowdiness. His extreme intelligence and sarcastic wit commanded respect from all of us but at the same time prevented him from acquiring bad grades, which were a sort of prerequisite for inclusion in the Group.

The clear memory of that day lives deep in my hippocampus, the black part of my brain. The darkness of it has not come from some fetal night, but from the events of that afternoon.

"Gentlemen, to the Clinic you have to present yourselves with a fever," I started the discussion. "The increase in temperature has to be stressed in the doctor's letter to the school. Only that could save you from the shit of harvesting hops." Lubos stared with an open mouth. Pepik nibbled on a pimple. Kaja picked his nose, in concentration.

"How to induce the fever, losers like you might wonder," I continued. "There is a sure and little known procedure: sterilize a sewing needle over a burning match. Thread it with a thread about five inches long. Soak the thread in gasoline. Then an intimate friend should pinch and lift the soft skin of your underarm, and you would penetrate the skin-fold with the needle and lead the gasoline-soaked thread through the tissue. Very slowly!" I could see that my description of the procedure had made an impression. Lubos Hanzlik put an unlit cigarette in his mouth, where it remained hanging, glued to the lower lip.

"The fever will appear in approximately twenty minutes and will last long enough for a visit to a physician. It will subside before you can reach the sanctuary of *"Na Kulatem Namesti"* beerhall on the way home. End of lecture, my fellow morons." Kaja and Pepik nodded with appreciation. That's how it has always been: we nodded in agreement on all the important matters. We understood each other; we were friends, loyal to each other, loyal as losers must be at all times. I could never detect any insecurity (the major curse of mankind) which would have driven a man to any achievement. I liked them all, their faces adorned by a sneer even in revelry.

"And how about the hot potato method, *vole?*" Lubos Hanzlik remarked. "You know, you heat a potato, put it in your pocket, and when they give you the thermometer in the clinic, and when nobody is looking, you stick it into the hot potato, *vole*. How about that, *vole?*" There was no response. "Or how about smoking a cigarette soaked in vinegar and dried—you'll get real sick, *vole*. I've heard about a guy who died like that, smoking three, he wanted to...."

"Lubos, shut up! Stupid stuff," Pepik Pycha ordered, and raised a hand to command attention. He got it. "Picric acid method—it has been well tested by army recruits. You know well about their desperation, you guys! One teaspoon of the powdered picric acid in a cup of milk, down it—and the next day the white of your eyes ain't white no more. The doctor will see nicely yellowed eyes, *icterus* they call it, jaundice. And you know what that could mean? Infectious hepatitis!"

Pepik made a gesture with his hand, cutting his throat. "Show me a doc who would risk not writing you a nice letter for the school: rest in bed in peace, and fluids. No fucking hops. Amen." Pepik Pycha rested, nodding in approval of himself.

Kaja Fot imitated a vomiting sound, asking for attention. That was his way. The curls of his strangely orange hair (long before punkism) still showed, on his temples, a little of the blue tint caused by a shampoo stolen from a friend of his mother's who visited their house. Too late he had recognized that it contained a blue dyeing component. The corners of his handsome lips were turned downward to suggest that his contribution would be serious, no pun.

"Gentlemen, *volove!* The sewing with gasoline thread and the picric acid cocktail are interesting proposals, indeed. But listen to the ultimate in medical deception!" He put the palms of his hands together as if in prayer. "Pay attention, screwballs, since you are in great need of guidance." He turned his head from side to side with an expression of resignation, then he laughed briefly and continued.

"All you need is garlic and band-aids. Yes, garlic. Mash a clove with a pinch of salt. Apply a small amount—about lentil size—to the skin on the belly and cover with the band-aid. Place a few more on your decrepit trunk. Maybe one on your ass, Lubos! Go to sleep, alone—Pycha, you would have no problem with that. When you wake up, take the garlic off. And *voila!* There would glitter a sparkling clear blister under each band-aid."

Kaja spread his arms, asking for appreciation. "This is what we call an ingenious deceit, in the business, yo-yos. The doctor would never, ever fathom the nature of your mysterious affliction. No fever, tongue pale, eyes bloodshed normally, balls shriveled as usual. But all those suspicious lesions?" Kaja turned around, looking out the window to demonstrate disinterest in our reaction.

"That's good, *vole*," said Lubos Hanzlik.

"Wow!" Said Pepik Pycha, his mouth remaining agape.

"Very cool," I might have said. "But let's ask somebody else. Let's ask Osten, there, what he would think about that. He's got the brains!" I turned around and motioned with my hand to Josh Osten, who was still scribbling something in the front row. The guys nodded. "Yeah," somebody agreed.

I remember the voice of Lubos Hanzlik clearly. It had a curious pitch that did not fit well his six-foot-three bulk. He turned around and called: "Hey, Jew Osten! Hey Jewboy!"

There was a long silence. Nobody said anything. None of us did anything then. None of us.

That was five decades ago, almost a lifetime. Not only my brain but also my heart remembers clearly. The memory is unkindly lucid, untouched by time, which has elapsed in haste without helping me to understand.

After that day our Group disintegrated, because we felt uneasy looking into each others' eyes. Kaja and I became friends with Josh Osten, who did not know bitterness. He had an aunt who was the director of the Jewish Museum in Prague and sometimes, somehow, Osten could get the keys from the building. We would sneak in there at night, and with all those wonderful ancient things around us we would play records of Tchaikovsky with vodka, and of *West Side Story* with rum. The young ladies we used to take with us were amazed by our sophistication and, therefore, were kind to us. The images of their kind deeds were encoded into the sunny part of my brain with great clarity. Still, today, they radiate like beautiful wild flowers on the confused landscape of my senility.

These are the brainwaves of memory I choose to surf into my sunset, leaving the "man in the grey suit"* of dark thoughts deep down in the deep.

---

* "man in the grey suit": shark, in the slang of Australian surfers.

Romancing "Platino"

He crouched in the bathtub, splashing water on his torso with interruptions that allowed the water to evaporate after each splash. That way it took only about twenty minutes to cool down using that tepid, rusty fluid. (In the thousand square miles of lowland tropical forest around the town Jjoro, the word "cold" could be applied only to the contents of two refrigerators: One belonging to the "rich man" and the other to the priest, both men of ominous reputation and both the size of refrigerators.) Bushek felt good. The bath rid his skin of its boiled-lobster hue, took the mad red glaze off his eyeballs, and retracted his tongue to where it belonged.

He put on his boxer shorts with the pictures of fawn-colored boxers on them, and made a cup of Nescafé with his coil heater, boiling the water for a few minutes in the self-delusion that the boiling would kill all waterborne pathogens. It was a matter of discipline to him. He had learned to be cautious about these things in the tropics, since even a runny nose presented a problem, with no long sleeves to wipe the nose. He took his cup and cigarette onto the balcony of his "hotel" room and settled there next to the giant wasps' nest.

The wasps liked him. They were coming in now with the breeze from the river. Down on the shore, the washerwomen were just finishing their toil, taking the laundry from the brown, muddy stream spotlessly snow-white. He wondered how it was possible and marveled again about the physical perfection of these athletes, enhanced by the wetness of their "*ropas*," or old-fashioned underwear, worn for this laborious occasion.

The rain forest across the river turned to a dark silhouette with the sundown, and the silhouette threw a sharp shadow on the river, on half of the river. It divided the stream in two: one pure black, and parallel to it a silver stream that shivered as if alive. Bushek got his flat flask, added a shot of Ron Viejo to the coffee cup, and toasted the sunset. "To the pancake," he said aloud—and the sun was gone. All of a sudden a black velvet curtain had fallen over that theatrical stage, over the Atrato river, over the jungle behind her, and over the washer-women. It was the curtain-down of an equatorial dusk-without-dusk, the night. It was time to yield the balcony to the night-biting mosquitoes with their miniature malaria-filled syringes. It was time to eat one mango, two bananas, one quanabana, and a piece of melted chocolate bar: dinner. Then to a bar near Calle Kennedy to shorten the evening, to forget about "chocoa," and to see the faces of people.

Bushek Ruzicka, Ph.D., was a biologist searching for a frog. The local Indian name for this two-inch-long creature is "chocoa," and it is well known and prized by the Cholo Indians for the poison it sweats from glands in its skin when impaled alive on a stick and held over a fire. The tips of split bamboo arrows for a blow-gun, *cerbatan*, are rolled over the skin of the unfortunate creature and thus coated with the poison. The poison is prized for its usefulness, because it is so immensely potent that a scratch with the tip of such an arrow will kill a man in a few short minutes.

Bushek's task was to collect a few of the blue and yellow frogs for experiments at the National Institutes of Health in Bethesda, Maryland. He had been sent to Colombia because of his experience in surviving the hardships of the jungle and for his proficiency in Spanish. Being forty years of age, unmarried, and childless also made him a good candidate as an eventual sacrificial lamb. He knew about the reasoning of his superiors; therefore, he had never revealed his love for the adventurous tropics, which might, somehow, disqualify him. On the contrary, he often loudly exaggerated the dangers and hardships anticipated in such a solo expedition. Now, in Jjoro, he was secretly content, almost happy at times, because everything around him was interesting.

The owner of the bar called "Boringen" was a cheerless character of Falstaffian proportions, with only one memorable attribute. His mass of abdominal fat had not grown into the splendor of a potbelly but had descended down into his pants, forming two jelly-like shivering pillows above his thighs, strangled and held down in place by the belt of his bellbottoms. He moved slowly, shuffling his feet, not as a result of his physical oddity but rather as a consequence of a chronic tropical dourness, matched by the lack of any expression on his baggy-eyed face, at all times. He never talked in sentences, only in gnomic utterances and single words with exclamation marks. He ruled over two waitresses, but he himself served a selected few customers including the "*gringo tipico*"—Bushek Ruzicka.

His bar extended onto a covered porch, elevated a few feet on stilts, which faced the mud of the intersection of Calle Medellín and Calle Kennedy. This position made "Boringen" a good people-watching spot and therefore Bushek's favorite watering hole. Besides, the place had been newly decorated. A larger-than-life poster of Silvester Stallone hung behind the bar, next to a framed original of the Mona Lisa, and another wall was adorned by the irony of a Swiss Air poster of an Alpine fairytale, complete with icefalls, snowdrifts, and cornices. In places, brown moldy growths on the poster disturbed the whiteness of the glacier.

Bushek found a table of rough-hewn *lirio* wood, right by the corner post, next to the railing under the "Alps," and ordered "*uno tinto*," a cup of black coffee. He was resigned to the fact that coffee anywhere in Colombia is a watery, acidic concoction, devoid of any aroma. (Coffee beans there are roasted, ground, and stored for ages in bags that cause its aromatic oils and resins to evaporate and sublimate.) He drank it anyway, according to the rule that "when in Rome (Jjoro), do as the Romans (Colombians) do."

For the same reason he ordered a shot of *aquardiente*, of "Platino," the local brand of this vile-tasting distillate, the only booze available. (To express, in public, a negative opinion about that anisette-flavored alcohol would amount to an act of treason, surpassing denigration of the flag, the president, and the nation.) So he had a sip. And ordered another one, waving his hand, since his voice would be unheard. The music from a boom-box on the bar blasted one song after another, without interruption: salsa, rumbas, sambas—and in all, the words "*amor*," "*corazón*," "*pasión*," and "*dolor*" were repeated and repeated in passionate howls at one thousand decibels. Real *dolor* in the neck, after a while. *Cantos from Hell*, Bushek thought, and managed to swallow his Platino.

He watched the ladies of the night commence their appearances. Like ghostly shadows, they passed Boringen to congregate along Calle Kennedy for their night shift. Their modest clothing did not distinguish them: no miniskirts, no micro-tanktops like those of their big-city colleagues.

A pair of lovers passed, holding hands, then a pair of drunks with their hands in the air, then the local feebleminded microcephalic ran by, emitting sounds. The unsmiling owner of the bar put another despised *aquardiente* on the *lirio* table with a splash. It had started to rain, and the intersection in front of Boringen was vacant of all living souls, save a few bats—acro-bats, which failed to cheer up Bushek. At least the heat of the day had abated.

———

Three dark silhouettes appeared on the corner. Bushek recognized them by their posture and movements—only Cholo Indians from the distant jungle, far up the Rio Atrato, then the Rio Capa, then the unnamed stream—move that way. They are small people, packages of carefully harnessed energy. They move in erect and even motions whether on flat ground or over rocky rubble or a fallen tree. They flow effortlessly, without a change of pace, without a bounce, like water over the smooth boulders of the upper Rio Capa, and always soundlessly.

They were heading toward the river, where their dugout canoe waited for them, no doubt. They would paddle and pole it upstream, to their home, *shabono*, all night and all day without stopping, without sweating, without any splashing or turbulence in their wake. As they reached the intersection, Bushek recognized the two males and a female walking a few steps behind. They all had identical Cholo haircuts with bangs covering their foreheads, their wet hair forming shining black helmets. The men, barefoot, wore ragged pants (they put them on for their rare visits to town) and their upper bodies were bare. They looked straight ahead, not to lower themselves by showing an interest in "civilization." The men were entering the glow of the swinging lightbulbs of Boringen's porch, not giving the bar a glance.

Then the woman became illuminated, passing a mere several feet from Bushek's table and eyes. Her *robe de soir* was only a wraparound of nondescript cloth around her hips, and a string of bead-seeds around her neck. Her torso was lacquered to a high gloss by the rain; her breasts pointed ahead to the river and slightly up to the sky. The best of *National Geographic*. Now, reaching the closest point to Bushek, she turned her head and looked at him.

Bushek winked an eye at her. In that instant he felt shame, blushed, perhaps. Like a used car salesman, he had actually winked an eye; *how cheap, how corny could he be,* he thought. But that took just a fraction of a moment.

She smiled at him, a wide smile, full of pearls. She was plain beautiful. She bit her lower lip and raised her eyebrows in playful rowdiness. She didn't slow down, proceeded in stride and turned her head away and disappeared in the darkness, like a shooting star leaving no trace, just wonder. A gust of wind misted Bushek's face. He remained motionless for a long while.

He spread his arms, inhaled deeply, and joined the salsa tune from the radio: "*mi amor me da dolor en mi corazon quando te . . . la la la.*" He talked to himself: "This one has a nice melody—and what a rhythm!" He paused. "What got into me, for Chris' sake?" He looked for a waiter.

"*Platino, por favor. Y uno tinto!*" he yelled.

The owner of Boringen's nodded and delivered, with an expression of conspiracy. Bushek looked at his face and turned his head from side to side. Surprised, he discovered a little kindness about the fat man's baggy eyes and the jolly tremble of his triple chin. So Bushek thanked him and told him he liked his place. Good bar. Good drink, your Platino. The owner of Boringen smiled, actually smiled.

Bushek sipped the liquor. After all, there was something about this *aquardiente,* this "Platino." It was smooth, one could not deny that, and it has quite a pleasant aftertaste, that's for sure, he mumbled. And the coffee, *tinto,* ain't that bad either: strong, and when one can sweeten it—good stuff. How come he had not noticed before? He downed the Platino, gagged, and chased it down with coffee. And the music; some really are melodious tunes, one has to admit, in all fairness. "I have to admit that," he said to himself.

Bushek listened to the percussion solo of the rain on the corrugated tin roof. He noticed the *Ravinia musicalis* palm bending in graceful curves with the wind across the street. He applauded the couple and their two kids dancing on the porch of the shack on the corner, the mad dance of moths around the light bulb, the balmy coolness of the rainy breeze bathing his sweaty hide. Bushek inhaled deeply. The air expanded his chest, and he felt like singing again; he had to restrain himself. He had seen the smile of the Cholo girl, the raindrops on her breast, her wild beauty; fun. He didn't need to close his eyes to see her clearly. He could not get the happiness off his face.

The rain stopped, as abruptly as it had begun, and the smell of open sewers returned, diluted. Not a cologne, but tolerable. People walked by the bar again. Somebody unknown waved a greeting at

Bushek, as one would greet a happy-faced stranger. Somebody else smiled at him. They did not know, of course, what single event of importance had taken place during the rain, to cause the pale male stranger to love all the world around him. The moon was breaking through the clouds now, making everything on the intersection of Kennedy and Medellín luminesce in jungle green.

African Apology

Reaching the sparse shade of the cannonball tree by the fence, he tripped on a root and, as if shot, sank to his knees, stumbled with flailing arms; then somehow his legs jutted from under him forward—and he recovered. Obscenity! Sweat covered him; his wobbly legs regained the pace again. There was the Bulumba Hospital! Another hundred yards and he would make it. Enough energy was left to increase his speed to pass the armed guards by the gate, swiftly but without running, of course. Jacob gazed straight ahead, avoiding any eye contact with them, which could induce a show of power, i.e., demands for documents, interrogations about the purpose of his visit, the third degree with an air of grave importance.

It had happened the last time he had come to the city hospital with his intestines in disastrous shape. The runs had lasted for a week and, finally, made him so dehydrated and decrepit that he had started to worry about harboring amoebae in his unfortunate gut. This time he was almost sure it was malaria, and he suspected it could be the malignant type, resistant to everything except the toxic Funsidar. It is known as "Blackwater Fever," to wide-eyed readers of romantic novels about colonial times. "Blackwater" not because the transmitting mosquito breeds in the black waters of secret jungle pools, but because the water the patient passes is as black as his or her destiny.

Jacob's knees almost buckled under his featherweight as he relaxed after negotiating the hospital gate. The attack of fever was over now, but it left his muscles feeble and his reflexes retarded. He had been bathed in sweat since midnight, half asleep, half in a state of semiconsciousness. Phantasmal caterpillars of elephantine dimensions and with multiple eyes had encircled him. They'd discovered his hiding place and were closing in at the moment when a sudden dawn silenced the village roosters and jungle sounds. The lack of noise woke him up. The nightmare had somehow persisted, even when his eyes were wide open, but he managed to exorcise the evil image by forcibly visualizing a picture of his wife and daughter back at home watching snowflakes melting on the window pane. He managed to bring the image into clarity.

His domestic, cook, and guardian angel Onuaku had come and given him fresh juice from a water-coconut and made the diagnosis of malaria with the authority of a Professor of Tropical Diseases. She had ordered the visit to the hospital. Jacob hoped now that the inevitable chills would not start again for a while, at least not while he was in the hospital, and that his friend Anezi, good Dr. Okeke, would fix him up with a cure—fast-acting, maybe Funsidar. And Anezi would tell him about hope and trust in modern science, and again about the beauties of immune surveillance, and his new girlfriend from Abua and the pleasing dimensions and poetic shapes of her body parts.

The last few weeks, Jacob had been counting the days remaining until his departure from Africa, as draftees do nearing the end of boot camp. It had been a long year. Two months ago, his wife and ten-year-old daughter had had to leave, and he had become lonely, some evenings painfully lonely. He had helped his adopted village to double the birthrate of goats, organized a new regime for feeding them, and got the village a new water pump. He had been useful, "making a difference" (as they would say in the Agency), and so he rejoiced in the belief that this pink-white man had been appreciated.

Sometimes he loved his villagers; most of the time he just liked them, and he knew he would miss them. But it had been a hard year. He had survived only by willing himself to be an all-terrain man, accepting local ways. An "old African hand, kid," he had imitated Bogart's slur in his evening monologue. His evenings were mostly monologues now.

He felt light-headed and as if floating above the gravel path between the bougainvillea bushes. Their poisonously purple blossoms seemed to be reaching for him; it took some effort to stay in the middle of the path. Two Housa tribesmen squeezed by him, holding hands.

Their eyes asked whether the white man was drunk or sick. Jacob felt both. He managed a smile, the universal greeting in cases of linguistic failure, and floated farther.

The hematology labs were somewhere in the left wing of the hospital, which consisted of a collection of bungalows connected by pathways. Some pathways were flanked by railings, and all were covered by corrugated sheet iron against the daily downpour of the tropical rainy season. Some corridors crossed; a few ended nowhere, connected to an imaginary building hoped for in the future. Jacob became confused. He remembered vaguely that Hematology faced a large jacaranda tree.

> Jacaranda,
> just to your name
> I will dance
> a pirouette.

He hummed his verse and, losing his concentration, he lost the way and ended near the wrong jacaranda, the one facing the hospital's garbage dump. Hunched vultures, squatting in the branches, stared at him without much interest, since he was still alive. They looked as if they themselves exuded the stench of the dump, one holding a bloodied gauze in its beak, another clutching a light bulb in its talons. Jacob turned away from the sinister scene and wandered over the grassy space between corridors. Some lepers, always in a group because of their state of social death, stared at him with interest, since he was still alive. An occasional nurse gave him a suspicious look. The flaps of their blue and white hats moved as if these black angels' wings propelled them to their desperate destinations.

Aware of his audience, Jacob straightened up and tried a look of determination, but found it difficult to combine with the appearance of nonchalance, a must for a foreigner who finds himself in a predicament here. Like an actor successful in covering up a forgotten line with an exaggerated gesture, his body language finally satisfied him, and his confidence, corroded by his surreal night of malaria, regenerated. He looked at the sky. A pair of hornbills jetted by with a shriek of greeting, and a few optimistic raindrops fell on his face, much welcomed by everything alive after the drought.

"I'm sorry!" Jacob almost collided with a man in an antique colonial pith helmet. This headgear was now rarer in independent Africa than slavery in the Niger delta, still today. A smile broadened the man's most peculiar, almost eccentric face. The Bantuic negroid features of a West African were covered by skin whiter than Jacob's, even with a reddish tint. An African albino, with a wide, inviting grin.

"*Nde wo*," Jacob greeted.

"*Nde wo. Kedo,* sir," the man replied, and switched a wooden board he carried from his right hand to his left. "How did you guess, sir, that it would be appropriate to greet me in Igbo?"

"Because of your smile, I guessed."

"Ha! Right you were," the man looked amused.

"Not because of your pith helmet, you know," Jacob said. "One doesn't come across any of those, nowadays."

"Well, Doctor tells me it saves my life, this thing from the good old times," the man said, pointing to the helmet. "You see my condition? I am an *anyale*, albino, you would say. Not wearing a hat, I would have had a nice funeral, long time ago, Doctor tells me." The man paused, still smiling.

"I would hope not," Jacob contributed.

"You know: skin cancers from the sun. Sad thing for an *anyale*."

"Sad indeed. But you are in good condition, Mister."

"Chinuo, my name, sir. I am the carpenter for the hospital."

"Jacob. I am with malaria. Perhaps." They shook hands and looked for words for a while. Jacob pointed to the wood in the carpenter's hand.

"Nice material. Nice-looking wood!"

"Cutting board, for the kitchen. The women there wanted one," Chinuo said.

"The little green in it—it looks almost like *afara* wood," Jacob tested, forgetting his search for Hematology.

"*Afara* is a nice-looking wood, and it has green in it, indeed." The carpenter spat on the wood and smudged it, "but this is camphor wood, sir, Jacob," he said. "It is the best for a cutting board."

"Really? Why is that?"

"*Afara* would crack in the dry season. And *iroko* would soak all the juices in; it would be difficult to clean. And soft woods? Well, you wouldn't even consider those."

"How about ironwood. That's pretty!" Jacob said.

"Oh, hard to get such a big piece of ironwood." He chuckled: "Besides, it would be too noble a wood for those lazy women in the kitchen." He spat on the board again, and they both watched the grain deepen.

"Camphor wood, you said?"

"Yes, yes. Quite a rare tree today. Villagers burn it for cooking, would you believe? They burn everything, you know." The carpenter smelled the wood as one would inhale the scent of a fragrant blossom. "It has oil in it, you see, so it will never crack in the dry season." He let Jacob smell it, too. "And not many know," he assumed an expression of importance and expertise, "that cuts in it will heal by themselves! Smooth like a baby's ass."

"Cuts will disappear?" Jacob exaggerated his interest. He liked the man.

"Yes sir, Jacob, the next day the cut isn't there. It has healed," he triumphed. They both touched the wood with admiration. "You came here for healing yourself, sir?" the carpenter asked.

"Oh, just that malaria. I think," Jacob said. "Got kind of lost. Trying to find Hematology."

"No problem." The carpenter pointed a general direction. They parted with customary greetings and with wishes of success for each other and health to their families. Jacob's spirit lifted after the discussion. The fatigue remaining from the night's fever felt almost pleasant now, as pain could please when not severe.

Soon the jacaranda tree, blooming in its dreamy blue, appeared. The hematology laboratories could be recognized behind it. Relieved, Jacob crossed the grassy space and approached the corridor running along the building. The last door on the right should have a nameplate with "Dr. Anezi Okeke" on it. Jacob imagined this cozy refuge. There he would find his old friend, and a cup of coffee and a bottle of Fanta lemonade right from the refrigerator. They would hug, talk nonsense first, then about his malaria, about the good old times in Minneapolis, the rough new times in Anezi's homeland and, yes, about his new girlfriend from Abua. Jacob speeded up his steps, in anticipation.

The corridor was elevated two feet above the ground with a banister three feet high. Seeing no other way to get onto the corridor, Jacob lifted his leg, reached up for the railing, and swung himself over it in one respectable move. Only his leather bag, which he carried over his shoulder, got caught outside the railing. He pulled it over and started walking. He almost stepped on a male agama lizard which crossed his path in panic. That was the moment the trouble started.

"What do you think you are doing? Climbing over the railing!" he heard behind him. He turned his head while still walking. A short fellow stood a few paces away, his arm in a questioning gesture. With the erect posture of a short man of authority, he was clad in a dark suit and tie. His face was very dark, his features suggesting the cunning intelligence of a "big man." Jacob could recognize a "big man" in an instant; his African experience had taught him the importance of this skill.

"Going to Hematology," he murmured, feeling immediately sorry he'd even answered the arrogant tone of the civilian whom he did not know, a stranger who had no business addressing him with a reprimand. Jacob continued walking away.

"Stop! I order you!" He heard an excited voice and continued walking.

"Stop him! Stop him at once!" This scream was obviously directed to a group of technicians, some in white coats who, indeed, lined themselves up in front of Jacob without much hesitation. Physically, there was no way he could walk further. He stopped.

Doors from the labs opened, and more people came out. He was surrounded. Jacob recognized one technician. She was of the Ibibio tribe, very pretty. They used to talk and joke together; she liked to use her English with him. Her eyes were elusive now. She showed no recognition of him. Nobody looked amused; a few talked in low voices among themselves, and when Jacob looked into their faces there was an embarrassed grimace, or their eyes were averted away.

"You should apologize to Professor, sir." An older man with a glistening balding spot said.

"For what?"

"You must apologize. For reason," the man stated dispassionately, in an even voice, without explaining the "reason." The others nodded their heads.

"Please, talk to Professor," an intense technician with an asymmetric face suggested, and tried an encouraging blink of the larger of his eyes. Somebody shouted from behind: "You have to!"

In Jacob's head a silent monologue raged, in sentences which cannot be revealed by a gentleman. It ended with the word "never." Jacob stood there, while a few people joined the Professor at the opposite end of the corridor and talked with him, some with agitation. Time passed.

"Would somebody call the security guard!" Jacob said, with hope for a resolution of this bizarre situation. "The hospital guard!" Security had official business around here; he could talk to them. He would explain that he had had to climb over the railing to the corridor—being lost. Is there a fine for that? Okay, then he would pay it. But apologize? To that "big man"? Ha!

"Somebody get the security guard!" he pleaded again, making his lower lip as stiff as he could muster. After a long while the crowd parted, and the guard shuffled in. His age was hard to tell, but he was an older man. His was the weather-worn face of a peasant, decorated with three parallel Yoruba scars on each of his sunken cheeks. A village man who, perhaps, had got a job as a security guard because he came from the same village as some high administrator of the hospital. The uniform hung on him sadly; the sleeves were too long, and the cuffs of the pants were dragging on the ground. The only respectable sign of his officialdom was the oily-black submachine gun drooping low from his shoulder.

Jacob liked him. A submachine gun carries authority over a crowd of white coats. The old guard did not speak English, so the intense technician translated for Jacob. The guard looked pained and worried, avoiding eye contact with Jacob, who explained that he had been in a hurry, that he had climbed the railing after losing his way. And that he needed to see a doctor, now. The guard decided, facing away from Jacob, that the white foreigner ought to apologize. Then he turned and, clutching his diminished authority, marched away stiffly, stepping on the cuffs of his pants. Jacob felt sadness for both the guard and himself. Then the guard turned around and returned.

"You should follow him, sir," the intense technician with the asymmetric face interpreted. The crowd separated, and Jacob walked behind the guard with the stride of a somnambulist, to the "big man's" office. The crowd followed, and part crowded into the office; the rest surrounded the doorway to witness this rare theater and the resolution of the last act. Who would surrender?

The short Professor loomed high behind his desk, by a hidden trick of upholstery. Jacob sat on a chair by the wall, erect with determination, aware of his innocence of any deed that would deserve an apology. There would be no discussion with the man behind the oversized desk with the ornate nameplate advertising his British degree. The "big man's" monologue, directed to both Jacob and the audience, was about somebody's misbehavior and arrogance.

"CIA agents, that's what you Americans send us!" he ended his raging, short-winded. It had gone over well with the crowd. Jacob was incredulous. "I want to see your passport!" the man ordered. "Somebody get it for me!"

Jacob did not move, and nobody from the audience dared to approach him. Jacob became aware of a Kafkoid turn of events. Yes, Franz would like this. "My passport is none of your business," Jacob spoke for the first time, loudly enough for everybody to hear. That was, perhaps, what enraged the "big man" into stuttering.

"Police. I'll call police." He grabbed the telephone and dialed the wrong number. Then he dialed again, but there was no connection. "You will pay for this, for this behavior!" he mumbled, dialing. "You will see our police." He dialed, mulishly, again, his finger circling the dial, followed intently by everyone in the crowd, which seemed to be increasing in number.

("To save face is more important than to save food"—proverb of the Greeks of Crete. "Respect is more important than life"—proverb of another bunch of losers, the Serbs of Bosnia.) Then a sudden realization of tragedy flashed in Jacob's mind. It brought up an emotion which caused him to breathe deeply and to sweat. His hand, involuntarily, lifted up to his forehead.

In the leather bag he clutched between his knees, there was a pouch with his passport, his return ticket from Air Afrique, and three hundred dollars in twenty-dollar bills. He had taken the pouch with him to the hospital because he planned to stop by at the Air Afrique office to reconfirm his return ticket. To possess, undeclared, three hundred U.S. dollars was against the strict customs laws of this country. On his travels to Africa, Jacob always carried this amount as insurance that he could use in a medical emergency, for a sudden evacuation, for a return to the world. To take it with him, together with his airline tickets, was an oversight, a grave mistake caused by his dream-like state after the malarial night.

Taken now to the police station, he would be searched; the dollars would be found and confiscated, and then the police chief would act on one of two options. The first option would be his imprisonment in the dungeon of a jail so atrocious that Jacob would not survive one week. Perhaps he could live two weeks. The second option would be the more likely one: he would be temporarily released, and then on the way from the police station, run over, accidentally, by a police car. Three hundred dollars is half the yearly income of a policeman, when not supplemented by criminal activities.

The image of Jacob's wife and daughter watching snowflakes melt on the window at home flashed in front of him like a transparency projected on a screen, a little out of focus. The level of suspense in the office-theater was such that nobody seemed to notice the rivulets of sweat running down their faces. All those bodies in the room increased the heat, while the humidity, enhanced by the silence, reached the saturation point. The rain started to rattle outside, and a dark beetle flew into the office from the doorway. Intent on self-destruction, it hit the window with the sound of a gun-shot.

Jacob stood up and approached the desk of the small "big" man in measured paces. He looked at the drooping entrails of the beetle smudged on the window. "I apologize." Nobody dared to banish the complete silence which followed. The "big man" laid down the telephone receiver and nodded his head, his face expressionless, like Jacob's. Then there were sighs from the crowd behind Jacob.

He turned around and, in a voice emerging with difficulty through his constricted windpipe, he quietly pronounced an obscenity. He adjusted the straps of his leather bag on his shoulder, straightened up, and walked away through the crowd, which separated, all still mute, wide eyes on him. Around the corner, near the entrance to Pathology, Jacob leaned on the railing and smoked a half-fill of his Danish travel pipe. Then he turned back and walked to Dr. Anezi Okeke's office.

"Sorry," Anezi welcomed him. "Really sorry." He had been informed.

"Well, fuck it," Jacob answered with a construct of a smile. He sat down. They did not pat each other's shoulder. Instead of old times and the girlfriend from Abua, they talked about Jacob's malaria. They parted with a courtesy not used by them before. Jacob promised he'd be back for a chat. Sometime. Anezi assured him he would be looking forward to it. Sure.

Leaving, the apologist looked at his watch. It was a quarter to ten, despite the heat. He wanted to think only about malaria, now, nothing else. The expected chills had not yet arrived, being still on their way. That was the good news, something to hold onto. But the pleasurable feeling of fatigue was now approaching pain. This pain freed the apologist from the shackles of recent memory, and blissfully occupied his mind past the armed guards at the gate, who grinned at him (they had been informed). The pain stayed with him under the cannonball tree with the roots exposed, on the way to the pharmacy, and then along the market to Ogu bus station.

A few kids ran behind him, laughing and clowning. They were led by a boy with a gun carved of wood with green streaks in it. It could have been camphor wood, which would not crack in the dry season. The boy pointed his gun at Jacob, the apologist: "*Oibo! Onya acha, onya acha!*" It was the usual: "English, pale eyes, pale eyes!" Perhaps, the boy had not been informed, yet.

Report on the State of Angels

(For Heathen Eyes Only)

Instantly, I knew these were angels; they couldn't be cranes. Realizing this, I became concerned about the question of my corporeality: Was I hallucinating? Was this a dream? Was I an authentic traveler? I took a peek at my hands, slowly bending then spreading the fingers. They moved normally, as I ordered them. The only trait that seemed to be out of the ordinary was the paleness of my nails.

I returned my gaze upward again, to face the unbelievable scenery, and readied myself to deal with this out-of-this-world experience, this celestial happening. They were converging from all directions, not unlike vultures or marabous seduced by the scent of carrion. Some walked, swaying from side to side, in the penguin way. Most flew in an unusual style: their bodies were not in a horizontal position, as in all flying birds, but hung down vertically. Two of the angels sort of skipped on clouds, flapping their twelve-foot wingspans to lift themselves up, then came down, jogged three or four steps, and up again. When they gathered around me, none of the angels was out of breath, and all smiled. The kindness and understanding that emanated from their angelic faces made me shiver, and I felt gooseflesh erupting on my cheeks.

They all wore uniforms, white acrylic nightgowns with a mock turtleneck fringed with faux-Belgian lace. There was not a ruffled feather on them, except on the wings. I realized their smiles were uniform, too, and permanent, unchanging, whether they whispered among themselves or when in flight, or now, when they gazed at me.

I smoothed my hairpiece and checked my fly, feeling like a lowly critter under the high-powered objective of a microscope. All I had were questions. They were my only possession. How did I get into this? What was my position here, high on a cloud?

The cloud, without a detectable silver lining, felt unexpectedly firm, as if created from styrofoam. It sounded hollow when I stamped on it carefully. A few angels noticed my move and nodded in an expression of empathy and benefaction. Soft tunes, molasses-like, oozed in from all directions except from beneath. Mantovani's elevator Muzak, filling the spaces between the polystyrene clouds and encompassing the smiling creatures, seemed to affect my stomach—but I was not throwing up, yet.

"God bless you, my dearest. But could you, please, reveal to us which passage you have traveled up to here? Which was your blessed route of ascent?" The angel who addressed me smiled, of course. She had hooded, watery eyes and colorless hair that flowed freely. Lusterless fuzz clung to her chin. Her translucency revealed a deficiency in melanin production. She looked exactly like the rest of the flock and, yes, the thought of cloning in heaven crossed the shrunken expanse of my mind.

"He did not crawl through the heavenly gate, as he should have; that's for sure!" Another angelic voice squeaked through the Muzak. I did not respond. *Jerk*, I thought.

All of a sudden a strange scene unfolded. All the angels collapsed on their knees, as if mowed down by a machine gun. They bent their heads in a submissive gesture, mumbling something I did not understand. Their reaction reminded me of the response of villagers to the arrival of a military governor in Nigeria that I had observed, years ago. Soon I detected the cause of their ingratiation.

A senior citizen with a flowing gray beard, in a long nightshirt, floated some distance across the sky. No wings on him, he moved as if he were on rollerblades, in a flowing motion. I could not see his face, but his general demeanor was that of a fellow well over his prime. I was almost sure that I was witnessing the passing-by of the god called God, or Lord, in whom a few Jews, many Christians, and even Mohammedans fiercely believe. I wished for binoculars. I wanted to ask the angel next to me, but she was trembling, so I did not.

Now was a good time to inspect the angels, undisturbed by their inquisition of me. If I was going to linger around here till eternity (a long time), I would be likely to get involved with a few of them, melanin or not. I know myself. Their kneeling, bent forward in their subservience, allowed me to judge the dimensions of their behinds. They did not have any! This observation sounds unbelievable, indeed, but I have not a single reason to prejudge this Report on the State of Angels.

God disappeared. They stood up again, allowing me to study the development of their other body parts. The shocking truth that I uncovered must not remain concealed: the growth and development of their chests was so minimal that any deviation from that of a male defied detection (and one could not blame only the heavy celestial fabric of their gowns). My decision formed instantly: *This is it! I have to get out of here, and fast.*

One creature approached me. "Maybe, my dear, you wouldn't adore it here," she said, as if reading my mind. "Adoooore," she said. "It would be much better down there for you, you know," she said, pointing somewhere to my feet, her wavering eyes looking sideways, away from me. "Lots of nice campfires; much warmer there, much warmer." She kept her vague grin.

Ha! An obvious conjuring trick! Such a glaring rip-off; I knew it right away. A simpleton's attempt at deception! No sir, this heaven ain't no place for Number One. I am a goner. At that moment, I felt a jolt in my chest, as if hit by a fist. Then another jolt. My knees almost buckled under me. I had no idea what was happening. The angels got foggy, out of focus as if observed through a cheap spyglass.

And then came the big one, a Mike Tyson. This third charge of electrical current toppled me down flat on my back. Everything blurred; the angels disappeared, and the sounds of celestial music changed into the wail of an ambulance siren. A bearded face appeared in front of me, with beautiful bloodshot eyes and a golden, saintly corona formed around his ruffled scalp by the ceiling light of the emergency vehicle. That unsmiling face filled me with a feeling of exhilaration and joy.

"Goddamn it, he needed three hundred fucking joules to get his ticker going, man." The bearded one removed the paddles of the defibrillator while watching the portable electrocardiogram recording the change from a boring flat line into the lofty peaks and deep valleys of life. He left the breathing tube in the patient's trachea in place, for now, and checked the oxygen and the blood pressure. All this was an automatic activity for him, but still it induced a prolonged rush of pleasure.

"Great job, Butch. That was a close one," the other man said. "Here. Here's the lidocaine. He's got good veins. How long's he been fibrillating?"

"Let me see. I can get it from the EKG here. Yup; over three goddamn minutes! This is the third one this month we brought back from wherever, Heaven or whatever, and I am counting only the fucking heart attacks, Ed. Only them heart attacks."

"Dynamic Duo, Butch, I'm telling you. We are some Dynamite Duo, boy!"

"Sure we are. That calls for a couple of pitchers in the 'Hurricane' tonight. How about that, Eddie?" He covered the chest of the patient with a blanket and winked at him, seeing his eyes open. The patient's eyes revealed that the mind was not at home yet.

The ambulance of the Florida Keys Emergency Service brought the victim of heart arrest to the Fishermen's Hospital on Vaca Key in six minutes. The patient's soul had spent three minutes of that six in a domain unknown to his saviors. Upon arrival at the emergency room, everybody went into action. Heparin was injected, blood was drawn, clot-busting "tissue-plasminogen-activator" was injected (one shot for $2,000), x-rays of the chest were done, blood pressure and electrocardiograph were monitored to tell the story of the heart continuously. A blood chemistry was done, assaying for GLU, BUN, CRE, ALP, TBIL, TP-, ALB, URIC, CHOL, TG, and others, including CKMB, which was judged to be elevated. Then a decision was made.

The patient was packaged in a blanket and rushed a hundred miles through the Everglades Swamp to Mt. Sinai Hospital in Miami, where the good doctor with the toothy Cuban smile, a master of marvelous percutaneous transluminal ballooning coronary angioplasty, at four o'clock in the morning, inserted a catheter into an artery at the patient's groin, threaded it up through the mighty aorta into the guilty heart, and then into the clogged left anterior descending coronary artery, the notorious "widowmaker," which the device unclogged like a roto-rooter, expanding it by ballooning it to a healthy width, and the patient felt like new again and, cocooned in multiple wires, EKG leads, and intravenous tubings, went to sleep with a smile on his face, dreaming of rum drinks under palms swaying in the tropically scented breeze.

The next day, the patient woke up rested, lucid to a degree ("the patient is in denial"), and free of pain. Beautiful angels floated around him, and he smiled at them. The angelic faces of the Filippino nurses returned the smile while they conspired to get for him a second serving of vanilla frozen yogurt, fluffed his blanket, tucked him in in a mother's way, touched his forehead and, checking his pulse, held his hand gently, as on a first shy date. When the patient told them that there are no prettier angels than the wingless kind, and that he was the Lothario who should know, they did not comprehend, and therefore giggled. They sneaked in the second serving of ambrosia (vanilla frozen yogurt) and pulled aside the windowshades so the patient could view the azure of Biscayne Bay.

When those gossamer blossoms of Asia were replaced by a shift of sturdy Russian emigrés, the patient asked for a sheet of paper and a pencil. He began to write:

Report on the State of Angels

Instantly, I knew these were angels; they could not be cranes. Realizing this, I became concerned about the question of my corporeality: Was I hallucinating? Was this a dream? Was I an authentic traveler?

Acknowledgment

The author is grateful for the support, in part, of his extraterrestrial excursion, to a "Grant in Aid" from The National Association for Near-Death Experiences, California. (Of course.)

How I Came to the Feast

The cause of my distraction is prosperity. It is everywhere around me. At some times it tranquilizes me to the extent of sleepwalking. It slows my movements as if they were filmed by a slow-motion camera. The abundance, the affluence.

My employer, Universität Giessen, has been endowed well, almost famously, even through recent times of leaner budgets, and therefore my lab lacks nothing. I can look forward to working, when I get up in the morning, in air conditioning set to a balmy 21° Centigrade, opening the refrigerator and removing lowfat milk and orange juice at 5° Centigrade, and pouring the milk over American cereal supplemented with enough fiber, vitamins, and trace minerals to "satisfy the recommended daily dosages." Every day I sin with a cup of freshly ground coffee, and off I go on my perfect machine, a titanium 21-speed mountain bicycle, on the paved bike path leading safely to the University. I pedal between the alleys of chestnut trees and through a park past the Goethe statue surrounded by flower beds, uphill between villas with rock gardens in bloom and a show of geraniums under each window. Everywhere I look, there is a tranquility and well-being. Some people I meet smile at me; some greet me with a waving hand—civility prevails. It is enjoyed, but without exuberation.

In a way one could be proud, being from Giessen in Bavaria, and most of the inhabitants are. I hasten to say that I appreciate it too; I do, indeed! But—my problem could be diagnosed as a recurring restlessness, as the urge to disappear to some malarian hole at the edge of a jungle, with sauna-like heat and humidity, about as healthy as a hospital sewer, under a leaden sky that pours five meters of water per year on the palm-fronded roofs of some sorry shacks sticking out of a permanent mudpie. Always, when I have managed to land in a defeated territory like that, I have felt such exhilaration and happiness that a conventional judge would assume I was wallowing on a topless beach in a Club Med with a Viper Key cocktail in my left hand and an incarnation of Brigitte Bardot supported by my right. And that, exactly, was the state of mind I attained trotting down the jungle path from the hills of the Golden Triangle on the Thailand side.

The forest was like a botanical garden, enchanted by singing and shrieking birds, butterflies the size of swallows, and beautiful beetles of bizarre shapes, the colors of gems. I stopped often, rested, and observed this curious world, the sweat and thirst only enhancing my feeling of adventure and, therefore, my exaltation. It was later in the day when I began tripping over the exposed roots because I'd lost concentration. My eyes were still watching the wet laterite clay of the trail, but my brain had started to turn over the kaleidoscope of images recorded during the past few days I'd spent up in the hills.

(The Lisu people grow the poppies and harvest them for the Karen people. They live in utter misery: diseased, scrambling for meager grub to survive. The opium dow is prepared by Karen tribesmen, who own the fields, tilled by the Lisu for almost nothing. The opium is bought then from the Karen by a solitary Hmong, who is ripping off the Karen expertly. The Hmong transfers the opium to a Chinese, down in Chiang Mai, who roars with laughter at the profit he's made from ripping off the Hmong. The stuff goes to a Thai military man who, of course, rips off the Chinese. And the Thai officer has further connections to the villains who make heroin from the raw opium. And the further way of heroin—that is a story too dangerous to know.)

I woke up from my ruminations to a strange noise coming from everywhere around me. It was an uniformly susurrant *shshshsh*. I stopped. I was not in the botanical riot of the jungle anymore but surrounded by a forest of slender trees of equal size, standing in neat rows about ten feet apart, obviously planted by man. The sound was coming from the tops of the trees, which looked like skeletons, almost devoid of leaves. Puzzled, I resumed walking and turned a bend in the path.

I almost ran into him, a white man standing there motionless, looking at me. He did not seemed to be surprised; he'd probably heard me coming. My first impression of him was his tallness, and the visor on his head. He must have been six-foot-six, in a bleached-out shirt with a Hawaiian design, shorts, and sandals. He had a leather visor on his head with a narrow shield as long as I have ever seen. It was a well-worn thing; sweat had made patterns on the shield resembling a horizon of mountain ridges. The wearer did not allow any frivolous tilt to it—the shield was pointing straight ahead, like a raven's beak, at me.

"Hi." I used the American greeting and smiled.

"Hi."

I stopped, took my eyes off him, and pointed at the tops of the trees. "What a strange noise!" I said in English.

"Yeah, caterpillars." By his accent, he was an American.

"Caterpillars?"

"Yes. The destiny of monocultures in the tropics," he said. I must have looked puzzled. "Yeah, they are eating the leaves of those teaks. They're almost finished. That is what you hear."

"Hah!"

"When millions of those microscopic jaws gnaw—one can hear it. I wonder how many millions we hear," he said. "Very interesting."

I extended my hand: "Lothar Burgdorf. How do you do?"

"I am Rick Gorlinski." He grasped my hand firmly. Rick was built quite impressively, sturdily; lanky tall, his spare movements gave the impression of power and speed, that his sinews held everything together tightly. His skin was sallow but darkened evenly, as goes with long stays in the tropics. He had not been suntanned on a beach. His unruly hair, of no particular color, was bleached rusty at the ends. One could see he was not in the custom of smiling readily; a suggestion of scorn was carved around his lips. His poked-in cheeks added to his stern look, quite in contrast to the pleasant, bright blue eyes flanking the beaked nose of impressive dimensions.

We walked together down to town, because he also was staying in Chiang Mai. Somehow, at first, his appearance made me cautious, and so I avoided small talk (to which I have an unfortunate affinity), at the expense of long silences. Slowly, our exchanges took the form of conversation. I learned that we were visiting the same mountain tribes of the Golden Triangle, but we did not go deeper into it. *Maybe later, if we could trust each other a little more*, I thought.

His home was San Francisco, which he had left almost two years ago. He had traveled through India to China, through the Philippines to Malaysia, before he arrived here in Thailand—for how long, he did not know. It was his rule to globetrot without rules, with one exception. Every morning, before he would set out on his excursions, he studied the local language. Later, it impressed me to hear him ordering our food in Thai and being understood. Thai sounds to a Western ear like gurgling, with lots of *krch-chrch*, and it pours out like an uninterrupted stream over sharp rocks.

From the first village, we were lucky to catch a bus to Chiang Mai. Darkness came with a near-equatorial rapidity at the time we arrived, and we entered the first lighted eatery at the outskirts of town. I ordered just a salad, since my German palate was sick of the spice that flavored everything here. Was it cilantro? Lemon grass? Fish sauce? It seemed to be in every dish I had eaten during the three weeks of my stay. And I did not want any more. Lately, I had become preoccupied with dreams about fresh rye bread with a crust, just butter spread on it, a glass of cold milk, potatoes sprinkled with chopped parsley—plain potatoes, the simplest. Rick seemed to enjoy the thick chicken soup with some leafy vegetable that emanated the smell of THAT thing. He seemed more relaxed after the soup, and we talked about his travels.

Then I told him about my interest in liver cancer and about my research in the university hospital here. I was collecting biopsies of tumors and setting them up in tissue cultures, forcing the cancerous cells to grow in flasks. Rick seemed interested in my project and asked many questions that revealed a surprising knowledge of the malignant process. Surprising, because he was a computer specialist by trade. We talked about remissions and prospects for treatment of cancer in the future, about mortality. Mortality?

"Sometimes death is okay, I think. Sometimes it isn't," he declared.

"Why do you say it is okay?"

"Not long ago, a good friend of mine died, you see. He fell asleep during some meeting. They pulled the chair out from under him, for fun. But he was already dead when he slumped to the floor. The 'falling asleep' was a massive heart attack," Rick told me, his gaze blank, seeing his friend perhaps. "That is an 'okay' death, I think. You see, for himself he did not die. Only for others: for friends, family. Not for himself."

"But he died. That is the sad fact!"

"Yes, but the last thing on his consciousness, the very last, was perhaps a vision of a shapely female, a pile of great food, or the smile of his kid. Isn't that what people visualize during meetings? So death, dying, did not enter his mind, even in the last second of his life—and then there were no thoughts any more."

"I understand—death without dying, simply an end of existence. Comfortable, great stuff! And it should be like that for people of any age—but the hitch is that for those who remain, for family, friends, the age of the dead one means much. That is the bad part," I said.

"I was thinking about that. One can draw a 'curve of ruin,' so to speak, a curve of the degree of devastation for those who remain. It might be relatively low at birth, rising and rising, then descending down again in old age. Would it make sense, you think?" He asked himself more than me, and continued: "I am Jewish, Lothar, so I checked in some old books from a rabbi, once. But I couldn't find anything explicit, blunt enough about this curve."

"Jewish or Catholic, no matter; ethicists, they would struggle with such a curve, I imagine. I think it would almost imply that over the age of, say, a hundred and under the age of one day, or before birth even, the curve would approach, or reach, zero. On both ends of your curve, death would mean nothing, no grief. How about that, then?"

"The sanctity of life! A sacrosanct concept—or a folly of Western man?" Rick raised his hand. He had a pleasant smile, a little sad though. I forced a laugh, thinking that we were deviating too far from anything resembling a pleasant discourse over dinner. "By the way," I said, "did you notice that girl who just came in?"

"I noticed her," Rick said dismissively, still in thought. "You know that the Eskimos, Inuit, have solved all this, in old times. They had it all figured out, what different values life has at which ages."

I ordered another Tsing Tao, Chinese beer, which tastes as bad as Miller Light— doesn't even vaguely resemble the brew at home in Bavaria. "Why the hell do we have to talk about death, Rick, with waitresses around like the one serving the back tables. Why? Have a beer," I said.

"Because. You know why?" He sighed and did not look very happy, at that moment. "I have been bumming around Asia for two years, I told you. That's why." I did not understand the connection. He topped our glasses, leaned back, and started to unbutton his shirt, from the top. I looked around, but nobody seemed to be paying much attention to us.

He undid the last button and opened the shirt so that his chest and belly showed. He had the suntan distribution of a peasant: the darkness of his neck descended in a V-like triangle pointing to his chest bone. The rest of his body was white. An enormous scar ran down from the edge of his rib cage, turned sharply across his belly, and disappeared sideways under the flap of his shirt, at least a half-a-foot long, down, and maybe a foot across.

"What happened?"

"Melanoma, my friend. My brother, he's a surgeon in Tucson, he took it out two years ago." Rick watched my reaction. "My dad is a doctor too. They couldn't guarantee anything—no way to know about metastases, about the risk that it will come back; nothing. Just the usual: let us hope." He paused, looked at the scar and then at me. "That was not good enough for me, so I sold everything and went to India and decided to travel till I'd either spent all the dough or had a relapse—and that would be it." His mouth smiled, but his eyes did not.

"But you look great; you are in great shape," I said.

"Well, I don't know. Can't sleep well for over a week now—I worry. Look here." He pointed at the scar. "See it? You are a cancer man, aren't you?"

Right in the middle of the scar there was an elevated lesion covered with a scab, a little wet with lymph. It was surrounded by a pink halo. It was not too big, just about a couple of centimeters or smaller. "They told me in Tucson to watch for something like this." He started to button up the shirt. "It doesn't heal; seeps a little lymph, doesn't hurt, and it crusts. It ain't pigmented, though. But they said it need not be."

"How long have you had it?"

"It's been about ten days since I noticed that."

"Let's have another beer, what do you say?" I suggested, and Rick called the waitress over, the uglier one. "I think I can help you, Rick. You are in luck. At least I hope you are in luck."

I told him that, by coincidence, my friend in the hospital, a Thai surgeon, had spent five years in Germany studying and operating on skin cancers, and melanomas are his special interest. He might be the number one melanoma expert in all of Thailand. Great experience; nice guy, too. I knew he would be in the outpatient clinic tomorrow. So we would meet at the hospital in the morning, and I would arrange for Rick to be seen by my friend. First thing tomorrow.

I arrived at the hospital half an hour before my rendezvous with Rick, to set up his exam with the surgeon. Rick was already pacing in front of the entrance. He looked different without his visor, his hair combed, his clean khaki shirt crumpled a little, and in fancy cotton pants. He was tense but tried his smile on me; the effort to behave casually showed. I made the arrangements at the clinic (there would be no charge), came out, and told Rick to go straight to the clinic. I'd come back to meet him in front of the gate in an hour. I had to attend to some business in the lab, I told him, which was not true.

"It will be all right, man," I said, doubting it, of course; melanoma is a killer because of its rapid metastases. Everybody knows that. I went to the open-air hospital cafeteria, drank two cups, and fought the thought of starting to smoke again. I watched passing girls and the morning acrobatics of butterflies over the clusia bushes around. I did not identify the butterflies and did not register the proportions of the girls, paying true attention only to the arms of my watch which moved like an injured snail.

Even before the hour had passed, I went to the entrance of the hospital. Rick was just coming out. When he saw me, he walked to meet me slowly. In that instant I knew—his face was changed so much that he only vaguely resembled the person I'd left an hour ago; only his nose was the same. "So, how was it?" I asked, to break the silence. But he just took my hand and shook it as if we were old friends who were meeting each other for the first time after years. He nodded his head and held my hand. Then his face erupted into an enormous smile.

"Okay, let's go and get a morning Tsing Tao. I know a place near the market where they keep it pretty cold," I said. We took a short cut, trudging through a construction site, alongside a Buddhist wat in ruins, crossed the canal, and he told me.

"Lothar, it was an insect bite. An infected insect bite! The doctor took a scraping, checked it under the microscope right there."

"I'll be damned," I said.

"Great guy, your friend. It is absolutely certain; no need for a biopsy, even. Sonovabitch, he laughed at me. I am going to buy him a bottle of the best stuff I can find here. The best!"

We got our beers in the shade of a sprawling bougainvillea vine that covered all of the terrace of the "Happy Dragon," and Rick talked about his plans. When he went back home to California, he would look for a teaching job, some private college out in a small town in the hills. Artificial Intelligence, that's what he would get into; there is a future in it. And being an old computer hacker would help him too. And hell, he might even get married. We paid.

"Lothar, how about at seven, tonight? Do you know the Austrian place?"

"Austrian? Like—Austria?"

"Good, you don't know it. Then I have a surprise for you, *mi amigo*. Good," he said, beaming. He still could not get the grin off his face. Neither could I.

At seven-zero-zero, on the nose, Rick appeared in the lobby of my hotel. (I love when people come on time. It must be the German in me.) In olive slacks, a black shirt, and an off-white cotton parka over it, he looked twice the size of the people around him. I had my white jacket and shirt with an ascot—almost too colonial, too Graham Greene, I thought. But we were terrific, fabulously handsome, intelligent faces, in tremendous *esprit de corps*. We kept our posture straight and paced with military deliberation, as if awarded medals.

I thought about some of my culinary adventures of the past. There was the breakfast of pelagic palo-palo worms in Western Samoa, the sweet and sour pig's Fallopian tubes with stir-fried ovaries in Taipei, the marinated sea cucumber-holothuria in the Peng-Hu Islands of the South China Sea. I recalled the fish, cooked for twenty-four hours, in Chinatown in Yokohama. But tonight it would be different—it would be the good old times, the old Viennese times!

The last droves of fruit bats were passing low over our heads on their way to night-feeding haunts, shitting happily, and I worried about my jacket. But only for a moment, since my single-minded desire for food had overtaken my imagination. I could not believe that nobody had told me about "Grinzing," the Austrian restaurant, which was only a few blocks from my hotel. Surrounded by a bamboo-fringed tropical garden, it stood on stilts at least three meters tall. The structure was designed in the traditional Thai style, with a broad verandah encircling the house on all sides. Teak railings, teak paneling and pillars, teak ceilings—all were bathed in the balmy stream of air coming down from the hills for the night. The only obvious Austrian feature was a snowy damask tablecloth over each table, and the vase on it. Blossoms of hibiscus, rosa sinensis, elevated the class of the arrangement.

Before we'd even found a table, Rick announced, with mock formality, that he considered this evening a celebration and that everything was to be on him. How could I have objected? The menu read like a fairytale I knew would come true. And it did—on imitation Meissen porcelain plates, sprawling over the rim, the Wienerschnitzel of my youth. The thinly pounded breaded veal was fried to perfect consistency by a Thai hand, undoubtedly guided by the frowning ghost of my grandmother (let the gods endow her with eternal glory). It came with steaming golden potatoes sprinkled with melted butter and finely chopped parsley.

The cold cucumber salad, Gurkensalat, was of the optimal acidity and salinity, as I have known it from home. Yes, G. B. Shaw understood: "There is no love sincerer than the love of food." I loved it so sincerely when the dessert arrived. It was the world famous Sacher Torte, indistinguishable from the original pride of Kortner Strasse in Vienna. I had arrived in heaven, finally.

The majordomo, Herr Karl Prochaska himself, came to discuss the wine. He apologized for the limited selection from his wine cellar, but there was no agony in deciding about the vintage of an Austrian riesling, since all are delicious with food, be it in the tropics or an alpine chalet. He was a balding, short fellow of about fifty, with a swift smile, blotches on his forehead attesting to the might of the equatorial sun, with a Burgundy-tinted bulb of a nose, suggesting expertise in wines. Rick told me that Prochaska had married the Beauty Queen of Chiang Mai and stayed here, so she could be close to her relatives and would not fade. It was a festive evening, and before it was over even Rick had noticed the angelic waitresses who fluttered around in gossamer Thai silks as if suspended in the evening breeze, jasmine blossoms in their hair and smiles reserved only for us, we were certain.

So, that is how I came to a feast—and how I made a friend for years to come.